Mary Anne and the Library Mystery

**Other books by
Ann M. Martin**

Rachel Parker, Kindergarten Show-off

Eleven Kids, One Summer

Ma and Pa Dracula

Yours Turly, Shirley

Ten Kids, No Pets

Slam Book

Just a Summer Romance

Missing Since Monday

With You and Without You

Me and Katie (the Pest)

Stage Fright

Inside Out

Bummer Summer

BABY-SITTERS LITTLE SISTER series
THE BABY-SITTERS CLUB mysteries
THE BABY-SITTERS CLUB series
(see back of book for a more complete listing)

THE BABY-SITTERS CLUB

Mary Anne and the Library Mystery
Ann M. Martin

AN
APPLE
PAPERBACK

SCHOLASTIC INC.
New York Toronto London Auckland Sydney

The author gratefully acknowledges
Ellen Miles
for her help in
preparing this manuscript.

Cover art by Hodges Soileau

ISBN 0-590-47051-5

12 11 10 9 8 7 6 5 4 3 2 1   4 5 6 7 8/9

Printed in the U.S.A.   40

First Scholastic printing, February 1994

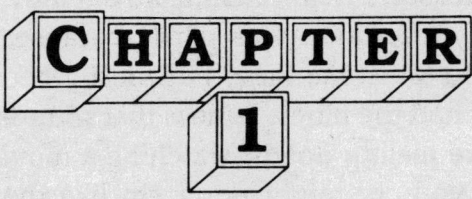

CHAPTER 1

At first, I wasn't really crying. I mean, my eyes *were* filled with tears, but I managed to hold them back. Not for long, though. Soon, the tears began to flow down my cheeks. I cried and cried, hiccupping between sobs. Finally I buried my face in the pillow I was clutching and just bawled.

Then the movie ended.

I wiped my eyes, blew my nose, and got up to turn off the TV. "Why do I do this to myself?" I asked out loud, sniffling a little. I end up weeping whenever I watch *Roman Holiday*, but I still love it. It's an old movie that stars Gregory Peck and the late, great Audrey Hepburn, and it gets me every time.

My name is Mary Anne Spier, and while I love old movies, I'm not a nostalgia nut. I also love rock and roll and the latest TV shows. I'm thirteen, and I'm in the eighth grade at Stoneybrook Middle School, which is in Stoneybrook, Connecticut — the town where I've lived all my life. I have short brown hair and brown eyes, and I'm not exactly tall for my age.

The reason I was watching an old movie that Monday afternoon was partly because I was trying to kill some time, but mostly because I kind of had the blues. I guess that sounds silly. If you're feeling down, watching a movie that makes you cry might not seem like the most brilliant thing to do. But somehow it made sense to me. I figured a good cry might make me feel better.

The only problem was that it hadn't worked. Oh, there was no doubt that I'd had a good cry. But as I headed for the bathroom to rinse off my face with a little cold water, I realized that I didn't feel one bit better.

I had been lost in the romantic world of *Roman Holiday*, but when I came back to Earth, nothing had changed. It was still a dismal, cold, gray day. I still felt bored and restless. I still missed Dawn and Logan, and Mallory, too. And it *still* wasn't time for me to head over to Claudia's for a BSC meeting.

I guess I need to do a little explaining here. See, I belong to this great club called the BSC, which stands for the Baby-sitters Club. All of the people in it are my closest friends, except for one. And that one happens to be my *boy-*

friend! His name is Logan Bruno, and he's extremely sweet and very, very cute. In fact, he looks just like my favorite actor Cam Geary, with deep blue eyes and a shy smile. He's from Louisville, Kentucky, and he speaks with the most delicious Southern drawl. Dawn, Mallory, and Claudia are members, too, and I'll explain more about them later.

Anyway, I love the BSC, and I always look forward to our meetings. But that day, I was *really* looking forward to our meeting. It seemed like the only bright spot in a very dull day.

I'm pretty emotional, as you've probably guessed. My friends tell me I'm the most sensitive person they've ever met. I cry easily, even when I'm not watching *Roman Holiday*.

But that doesn't mean I'm a *sad* person. Usually I'm cheerful and usually I really enjoy life. Being a sensitive person has its ups and downs, though. The *up* part is that people seem to find me easy to talk to, and when somebody is happy I can share his happiness. As for the down part of being sensitive, well, you know the end of the movie *The Wizard of Oz*? When everybody in Oz is saying goodbye to Dorothy? The Tin Man whispers "Now I know I have a heart, because it's breaking." (Of course, I go through a box of Kleenex during that scene.) What I'm trying to say is that being sensitive leaves me open to a lot of wonderful emotions, but it also leaves me open to some not-so-pleasant feelings.

And lately, I have definitely been feeling not-so-pleasant. As I said, I miss Logan and Dawn and Mallory. I miss Logan because he's on the volleyball team, and the team is in the middle of a tournament these days, and Logan is constantly busy with practices or games. Boo. I mean, of course I hope the team does well, but what about me? I miss my boyfriend.

As for Dawn, maybe I should explain who she is. Dawn is my best friend, and she also happens to be my stepsister. Here's how *that* came about. See, my mother died when I was just a baby. I never knew her, so I don't exactly *miss* her, but sometimes I do miss having a mom. I was brought up by my father, and basically I have to give him credit for doing a decent job. For a while, he was incredibly strict about such things as how I dressed and what my room looked like. But these days he's a little more easygoing.

So, there you have my dad, a Connecticut widower with one daughter. (I'm an only child.)

Enter Sharon Schafer, Dawn's mom. Like my dad, Sharon grew up in Stoneybrook. In fact, Sharon and my dad used to date each other when they were in high school.

Dad lost track of Sharon when she went off to college in California. She got married out there and had two kids. Then, when her marriage broke up, she moved back to Stoneybrook, bringing her kids with her. That's when she and Dad met up again, all because Dawn and I had become friends and found out about our parents' high school romance. It sounds complicated, but it isn't, really. Sharon and my dad (his name's Richard, by the way) fell in love soon after they started dating again, and not too long after *that*, they got married.

Sharon plus Richard equals instant family! For so long, it had just been Dad and me. But all of a sudden I had a stepmother, a stepsister who was already my best friend, and a stepbrother. That's Jeff, Dawn's ten-year-old brother. I don't know Jeff very well, because he didn't live in Stoneybrook for long. He had a hard time adjusting to life in Connecticut, and he ended up going back to California to live with his dad. Still, after the wedding, when Dad and Tigger (he's my kitten) and I moved in with Dawn and her mom, their old farmhouse seemed pretty full.

It's a really neat house. It was built in, like, 1795, and it's different than any house I've ever been in. It has small rooms with low ceilings, narrow stairways, a big brick fireplace in the living room, and best of all, a secret passage. Honest. This house used to be a stop on the Underground Railroad. Dawn is sure a ghost haunts the secret passage, and while she may be right, it's something I'd personally rather not think about. Dawn loves ghosts and ghost stories, but, to be honest, they scare me to death.

I guess I've gotten off the subject. I was trying to explain who Dawn is and why I miss her, wasn't I? Let me see. Apart from being my stepsister, Dawn is thirteen and in the eighth grade, just like me. She has long, long blonde hair and big blue eyes and a terrific approach to life. She's easy-going and tolerant, and she knows her own mind. Why do I miss her? Well, not that long ago, Dawn started *really* missing her dad and Jeff. Being a person who knows her own mind, she decided that she wanted to go back to California for a few months and live with them.

It turned out to be a good decision for her. She's having a great time out there, and I think she feels that her relationship with her dad and Jeff is much stronger now.

But it's *not* so good for me. Do I sound as if I'm feeling sorry for myself? Well, I am. Poor, poor Mary Anne. That's me. I'm just kidding — I think. In fact, I do miss Dawn a lot. I mean, losing your sister *and* your best friend at the same time is an awful lot to deal with. Especially when it's winter in Connect-icut, and everything is gray and cold and boring.

"I just need something *new* in my life," I told Tigger. I was lying on the couch, and Tigger was curled up on my stomach. He was purring contentedly. It doesn't take much to make a cat happy. "Any ideas?" I asked him, as I stroked his chin. He just purred more loudly. I sighed.

Oh, I forgot to explain about Mallory, the other person I miss. She's another member of the BSC, although, unlike Dawn and me, she's eleven and in the sixth grade. And these days, I haven't seen too much of her because she's sick with mono and has to spend most of her time indoors, just resting. Now, Mal isn't my best friend or anything, but I do miss her. The club just doesn't seem the same without her and Dawn.

I checked my watch. It was only four-thirty, and the BSC meeting wouldn't start for an-other hour. I figured I would leave my house at five-fifteen, even though it only takes me a few minutes to walk to Claudia Kishi's house, where we meet. That still left forty-five min-utes, and I had absolutely nothing to do. I stared at the ceiling, hoping for inspiration.

Just then, I heard a thump on the front porch. "That must be the newspaper," I said to Tigger. I lifted him gently off my stomach and put him on the floor. Then I got up and fetched the paper.

I have to confess that I don't read the paper every single day. I mean, I'm interested in what's going on in the world, but I can let a few days go by without brushing up on my current events. However, that day, I was so desperate for something to do that the paper looked fascinating. I took it into the kitchen, made myself a cup of hot cocoa, and settled in to read.

I saw the usual articles about all the terrible stuff going on in the world. I skimmed through those, since I didn't want to feel even more depressed than I already was. Then I saw a piece about a bus driver who had won the lottery. That cheered me up a little, and I took some time out to fantasize about what I would do with a million dollars. I read the weather next, but that brought me down again, since they were forecasting nothing but more gloom and clouds. I skipped to the editorials page and read through the letters to the editor. I always like to see if I recognize the names of the people who write. One letter was about how the school board needed to shape up, one was about banning books, and one was about how a Stoneybrook ambulance crew had saved someone's life.

I yawned and turned to the birth announcements. That's another section I like to check out, just to see if any kids have been given especially nice or especially weird names. Unfortunately, most of the names that day were normal and boring — no excitement there.

I read Dear Abby (*why* do people always write about how their husband or co-worker has bad breath? I mean, what's the big deal?) and the comics, and I skimmed the sports page to see if there was anything about the volleyball tournament. There wasn't. I was just about to start reading the want ads when I happened to glance at my watch. It was ten after five. "Finally!" I said. I decided to leave then and walk even *more* slowly to Claudia's. I couldn't wait for the meeting to begin.

CHAPTER 2

"**W**ow, *you're* early," said Claudia, when I burst into her room a few minutes later.

"And you've been *crying*," said Kristy. "Are you okay?"

I looked at myself in Claud's dressing-table mirror. Sure enough, my eyes were red and puffy. "I'm fine," I said. "I was just watching a movie."

"Which one was it this time?" asked Claudia. "*Little Women*? *Gone With the Wind*?"

I shook my head.

"Then it must have been *Roman Holiday*," said Kristy, grinning.

I nodded. Kristy knows me well. She's my *other* best friend. I've been friends with Kristy Thomas since before either of us knew how to walk or talk. You wouldn't think the two of us would have a lot in common — she's as brash and self-confident as I am quiet and shy — but I guess we complement each other.

Kristy is the president of the BSC, and she's a stickler for punctuality, which explains why she was already seated in her usual spot in Claudia's director's chair, ready for business, wearing her visor, a pencil tucked over her ear.

Kristy and Claudia and I sat and talked while we waited for the other members to arrive. I began to feel better. I forgot about being bored and lonely as I listened to Kristy describe a game her little brother had made up. Kids are so creative, and so much fun. That's why I love the BSC: it's all about being with kids. And the other members of the BSC love kids as much as I do.

I think that's the main reason the BSC works as well as it does. We run our club like a business, but if we didn't love what we were doing I don't think the business would be nearly as successful.

Maybe I should explain how the BSC works, and introduce the rest of the members. The original idea for the club was Kristy's. She's a real "idea person" and always has been, but *this* idea was one of her best. One night when her mom was calling all over the place trying to find a sitter for Kristy's little brother, Kristy had a flash. Wouldn't it be great, she thought, if parents could call one number and reach a whole bunch of experienced sitters? Well,

Kristy was right. As soon as we started the BSC, we found out that parents loved the idea, too.

The club meets three times a week, from 5:30 till 6:00, in Claudia's room. Parents call during those times to arrange sitting dates. It's that simple.

Well, actually, there's a little more to it. For example, we keep the club notebook. That's another of Kristy's ideas. Each of us is responsible for writing up everything that happens on every one of our sitting jobs. Then we read the notebook, and that way we can stay up-to-date on what's going on with our regular clients. For example, if Jamie Newton is going through a picky-eating phase, we all know it.

We also have a club record book, where we keep track of our jobs, and a treasury for the club dues. And each of us has a Kid-Kit, a box full of toys, games, and stickers that kids love to play with on rainy days. The toys and games are usually hand-me-downs, but they're new to the kids, and the kids love them. Kid-Kits were Kristy's idea, too.

After all the years I've known her, Kristy still amazes me. She's so full of energy and enthusiasm for whatever she's doing. And she does a lot. Besides being president of the BSC, she coaches a softball team for little kids. Plus, her family keeps her busy. Kristy has a big, complicated family. She grew up with two older brothers, Sam and Charlie, and one younger one, David Michael. Then, when David Michael was very little, Kristy's dad walked out on the family. Kristy's mom worked hard, and kept the Thomases going strong for years. Then she met, fell in love with, and married a really nice guy named Watson Brewer, who also happens to be tremendously rich. After the wedding, Kristy and her family moved across town to live in his mansion.

Watson has two children from his first marriage, Karen and Andrew. They live at the house part-time. And soon after Watson and Kristy's mom got married, they decided to adopt Emily Michelle, a two-year-old Vietnamese girl. Once Emily Michelle had arrived, Kristy's grandmother Nannie moved in, too, just to help out. All those people, plus the pets (Shannon, a Bernese mountain dog puppy, Boo-Boo the cat, and a couple of goldfish) make for a pretty chaotic household. But Kristy seems to thrive on the chaos.

Kristy looks a little like me, with brown hair and eyes. She's pretty short, too. But she's much more active than I am, and she doesn't care much about clothes or makeup. She's happiest wearing jeans and a turtleneck, and maybe her baseball cap with a picture of a collie on it. (The collie reminds her of her family's beloved first dog, Louie, who died a while back.)

"Where *is* everybody?" asked Kristy, after she'd finished the story about David Michael's new game. "It's almost time to start the meeting."

"Not quite," said Claudia, pointing to the digital clock on her nightstand. "It's only twenty-five after." Claudia picked up a scarf from her dresser and folded it into a cool-looking headband. "Chill, Kristy, they'll be here soon," she went on, as she admired her handiwork.

Claudia Kishi is the vice-president of the BSC. She gets to be VP because we meet in her room, and we meet in her room because she's the only one of us who has her own phone, with a private number. We could never tie up anybody else's phone the way we tie up hers.

Claudia is Japanese-American. She has beautiful long black hair, dark almond-shaped eyes, and a knack for stylish dressing. Claudia is incredibly creative. Her older sister, Janine, is an authentic genius, academically, but I happen to think Claudia is an *artistic* genius. It's true that Claudia doesn't do too well in school, but on the other hand I don't know anybody else who can draw or paint or sculpt or make jewelry the way she can. Luckily, Claudia's parents value her talents, even though they also wish she would "apply herself" and do better in school. Claudia's mother is the head librarian at the Stoneybrook Library, and she's constantly encouraging Claudia to read books that she feels are more challenging than the Nancy Drew mysteries Claud loves. In fact, Claudia is forbidden to read Nancy Drew books.

She's also not supposed to eat junk food, but you'd never know it. Claudia practically lives on things like Ring-Dings and Smartfood and Three Musketeers bars. She hides the stuff all over her room, but she's not stingy with it — she always shares it with the rest of us during meetings. Too bad the vice-president of the United States doesn't do that during *his* meetings. Maybe the world would be in better shape if our vice-president shared some Chee·tos with the heads of other countries.

One person who regularly turns down Claudia's offers of junk food is her best friend, Stacey McGill, the treasurer of the BSC. Stacey isn't a health food nut; she passes on the junk food because she's diabetic and has to be very, very careful about what she eats. Diabetes is a disease which prevents your body from processing sugar properly. Stacey has to monitor her blood sugar all the time, and give herself shots of insulin, which her body should produce but doesn't, at least not in the right amounts.

However, Stacey isn't a shy, quiet invalid, like Beth in *Little Women*. She's fun and outgoing and very cool. She grew up in New York City, and she still goes back there to visit fairly often. Her parents are divorced, and while Stacey (who's an only child) lives in Stoneybrook with her mom, her dad lives in New York. His apartment is, as Stacey says, "just a hop, skip, and a jump away from Bloomingdale's. How convenient!" Stacey is a champion shopper, and she has a great eye for trendy clothes that look terrific on her. She has blonde hair, permed most of the time, and bright blue eyes.

As treasurer, Stacey is responsible for collecting club dues and keeping track of our money. She's great at math, so she enjoys the job. None of us really *likes* paying dues, but the treasury is important. Without it, we wouldn't be able to help cover Claudia's phone bill, or pay Kristy's brother to drive her to meetings, or buy supplies for our Kid-Kits. We also wouldn't be able to have pizza-and-ice-cream parties, and I *know* we'd miss those.

I'm the club secretary. The record book is my responsibility, which means I have to know everybody's schedule and figure out who's free for what job. I also keep records on all our clients: names, addresses, emergency numbers, allergies, stuff like that. I love being secretary. To me, there's something very satisfying about keeping a nice, neat notebook. Dawn's always telling me that my dad and I are "neat freaks," and I guess we are.

When Dawn's not in California, she's the club's alternate officer. The alternate officer covers for any *other* officer who can't make a meeting. While Dawn's away, Shannon Kilbourne is taking care of that job. Shannon is usually what we call an associate member, which means she doesn't come to meetings but only helps out when we need extra sitters. Fortunately for us, she's agreed to become a full-fledged member until Dawn returns, so she does attend our meetings these days.

Shannon lives in Kristy's new neighborhood. She has thick, curly blonde hair, and sparkling blue eyes. She goes to private school instead of SMS, so only Kristy knew her well before Dawn left. I, for one, am happy to know Shannon better. She's really smart, and she's fun to be with. Shannon has two little sisters, Tiffany and Maria, so she's used to kids. She's a terrific sitter.

Now that Shannon is a regular member, we have only one associate member. That's Logan. He hardly ever comes to meetings, partly because he's an associate and partly because of team practices, but also because he's not exactly comfortable being the only boy in a small room with seven girls. Who can blame him?

I've already mentioned Mallory Pike, one of our two junior members. The other is Jessi Ramsey, Mal's best friend. I have a feeling that these days Jessi misses Mal as much as I miss Dawn. They're really close.

As junior officers, Jessi and Mal are only allowed to sit on afternoons and weekends, unless they're sitting for their own families. Mal, when she's well, usually has a lot of opportunities to sit for her own sisters and brothers, because she has *seven*! Adam, Byron, and Jordan are identical triplets; after them come Vanessa, Nicky, Margo, and Claire. The Pike kids can be a handful, but they're also fun.

Mallory and Jessi have a lot in common. They both love horses, they both love to read, and they're both very sure about what they want to be when they're older. Jessi intends to be a ballerina — and she's already well on her way, taking classes at a professional ballet school. Mal's going to write and illustrate children's books. She's probably spending a lot of her time thinking up plots these days, since she can't do much else.

As for looks, well, Mal has red hair, freckles, glasses, and braces. She's cute, but she sure doesn't think so. She can't wait till her parents let her get contacts and her braces come off.

Jessi is African-American, with cocoa-colored skin and the long, long legs of a dancer. She has a little sister named Becca and a baby brother known as Squirt. (His real name is John Philip.) Jessi's Aunt Cecelia lives with the family, to help out while Mr. and Mrs. Ramsey are at work.

So, that's the BSC. Sounds great, doesn't it? It is. I think I'd go crazy without it these days. By the time Kristy called the meeting to order — at precisely five-thirty — I'd already forgotten about the chilly, gray day and how lonely and bored I was. Stacey collected dues, since it was a Monday (that's dues day every week), and then we talked for awhile about one of our favorite clients, Jamie Newton. We skipped from Jamie to this scary movie we'd seen on TV the night before, and from the movie to a new kind of blush Claudia wanted us to try out. In between all the talking, the phone rang pretty steadily, and we lined up job after job.

At five to six, as the meeting was ending,

we heard a knock on the door. "May I come in?" asked Mrs. Kishi, peeking into the room. "I'm here on official business." She smiled.

"Well, in *that* case," said Kristy, smiling back, "come on in!"

Mrs. Kishi squeezed in next to Claudia, who was sitting on the bed. "I don't know if you can help me," she began, smoothing her gray wool skirt. "You may be too busy to take this on. But I am *desperate* for some help in the children's room at the library. We're having a Readathon to raise money to buy new books, and the place is going to be overrun with kids for the next couple of weeks. We need a volunteer in the afternoons, after school, and also on weekends. My staff is terrific, but they'll never be able to work with all the kids who have signed up."

I barely waited for her to finish speaking. "I'll help!" I said, the second she was done. This sounded like the *perfect* job for me. I love books, I love spending time in libraries, and I love kids. This job would be something new and different, just what I needed to get rid of my blues. Working at the library would be a zillion times better than watching old movies and crying all afternoon!

The meeting ended soon after that, but I stayed in Claudia's room, arranging a schedule with Mrs. Kishi. I would be working in the children's room a few afternoons a week, depending on which days they needed me most, and also on Saturdays and Sundays. The only bad thing about the Readathon, as far as I was concerned, was that it didn't begin that very minute. I could hardly wait to get started.

CHAPTER 3

Even though I couldn't start my new job right away, my blues were already gone. Having something to look forward to made all the difference. On Monday, a week after Mrs. Kishi had first asked for help, I reported to the children's librarian after school. Her name is Ms. Feld. She's the most energetic woman I've ever seen; she always seems to be in three places at once, doing five different things.

"Hand me that registration form, would you, Mary Anne?" she asked, after I had introduced myself. "Billy, please don't tear the heads off the puppets," she called to a boy playing in the puppet theatre behind her. "Miss Ellway, I think Jonathan needs some help signing out those books," she added, gesturing toward a little boy who was waiting at the main desk. She gathered up a pile of books, stuck a tape dispenser under one arm, and put the registration form I'd handed her in her mouth. "Thish way," she said, between clenched teeth, "we can talk over here." She led me to the office area of the children's room, which consisted of a few desks shoved together to make space for processing new books, repairing old ones, and doing all the other work that keeps a library running.

Maybe I should describe the children's room. It's on the first floor of the Stoneybrook Library. There are a lot of windows, so it's bright and sunny. Along with loads of wonderful books, the rooms (there are two of them) are full of cozy little nooks and crannies where kids can curl up and read. There are some tables, for homework or other projects, and lots of colorful posters are on the walls: illustrations from favorite children's books, mostly. The puppet theatre, which is painted bright blue and has yellow curtains, stands in one corner. A giant Raggedy Ann doll, big enough for a child to lie on or just snuggle with, sits in another. The main room is where the fiction is shelved. That's also where the office area is, and the main desk. A smaller room holds the card catalog and the non-fiction.

I feel at home in the children's room, even though it's fairly new (they kept the children's books upstairs when *I* was little). I guess something about the way a library looks and smells makes me feel comfortable and happy. Sometimes, I think I could just curl up with the big Raggedy Ann doll and spend days and days re-reading my favorite kids' books. I'd start with *Charlotte's Web*, and then I would read *Little Women* and its sequels, and *Little House in the Big Woods* and *its* sequels. After that — well, you get the idea.

"So!" said Ms. Feld, dumping her armload of books on a desktop that was already full of books, papers, and library supplies. "I'm delighted you could help us out, Mary Anne. I only have a few minutes to explain the Readathon to you, but I'm sure you'll understand. And you can always check with Miss Ellway if you have questions. She just started working here a couple of weeks ago, but she knows her way around. And she's been helping me get ready for the Readathon, so she knows all about the program."

I glanced over at Miss Ellway. I didn't want to have much to do with her if I could help it. I know I shouldn't judge people quickly, but my first impression of her (formed in about two seconds) was not a good one. For one thing, she looked unfriendly. She was tall and thin, with straight thin lips and straight thin gray hair and a thin, pointy nose. For another thing, she *acted* unfriendly. When Ms. Feld had asked her to help the boy sign out his books, she had sighed with exasperation, as if she were too busy with *important* things, and turned to the boy with a frown. "Where's your card?" she had asked him brusquely.

I looked back at Ms. Feld. She seemed so pleasant compared to Miss Ellway. Her curly brown hair looked a little messy, as if she'd forgotten to comb it that morning, and her sweater was missing a button. But when she smiled, the details didn't matter. Her green eyes lit up, and you could tell she loved her job and everything about it, even if it did keep her on the run all day, every day.

She smiled at me now, and I smiled back. Then she handed me the registration form she had carried in her teeth. "Why don't you look this over while I explain how the program works?" she said. "And while I explain, I'm just going to process a few of these books, if you don't mind. We're so far behind it's not funny." She began to paste pockets into the new books, stamp them with the library's name, and cover them with plastic that would keep them looking fresh. Her hands never stopped moving as she told me about the Readathon.

"Okay, here's how it works," she said. "The kids who want to participate fill out that form, which tells us who they are, what grade they're in, and how many books they plan to read during the weeks the Readathon is in progress. They sign up sponsors, who agree to pay them a certain amount for every book they read. We've made up a reading list for each level, so a third-grade kid would be reading from the third-grade reading list."

I nodded. It seemed simple so far.

"Each time a child finishes a book, he or she tells one of the staff members, and is given a brief quiz — just a few questions — to make sure he really did read the book. Then he receives a little certificate for each book read." She poked through a pile of papers on her desk and pulled out a certificate to show me. "At the end of the Readathon, the sponsors pay the kids according to how many certificates they've earned. The money goes toward our book budget, which can certainly use some help."

"Isn't there something about prizes, too?" I asked. I had seen a notice about the Readathon in the newspaper.

"Right," she said. "I almost forgot about that. At the end of the Readathon, we'll award a prize to the kid in each grade who's read the most books. The prizes will be things like ice cream sundaes, pizzas, and gift certificates, all donated by local merchants."

"It sounds great," I said.

"I think it'll be fun. But it's going to involve plenty of work. A *lot* of kids are going to be participating. It's so cold and gray these days, and they need something fun to do."

I could relate.

"So!" said Ms. Feld, slapping the last, finished book on the pile. I couldn't believe how fast she had worked, especially since she had been talking to me the whole time. She stood up. "Ready to get started?"

"Definitely," I replied. I followed her back to the main desk, and she introduced me to Miss Ellway.

"Mary Anne's going to be helping out with the Readathon," she said. "I told her to come to you with any questions, but I don't think she'll have too many."

Miss Ellway looked me up and down. "I suppose I'll have to show her how to use the card catalog," she said in a weary voice.

"That's okay, I know how," I spoke up quickly, trying not to sound annoyed. I mean, for one thing, I've known how to use the card catalog since I was about eight years old. And for another thing, I'm not crazy about being referred to as "her."

Ms. Feld gave me a comforting smile. "Of course you do," she said. "But you know what? I see somebody over there who *doesn't*." She winked at me and nudged me toward the card catalog. It was time to start my new job.

As I walked closer to the girl standing at the card catalog, I realized I knew her. "Hi, Corrie," I said. "Need some help?" Corrie Addison, who's nine, is one of the kids the BSC sits for. I had a feeling I'd be seeing a lot of our clients in the children's room.

"Hi, Mary Anne," she said. "I'm trying to find a book about mummies. The Readathon list says I can read up to ten nonfiction books on any subject I'm interested in."

I jumped into my new role. "Okay," I said. "Here's how we can do that." I located a particular drawer, pulled it open, and leafed through the cards until I found what we were looking for. "Here we go," I said. "There are four books listed here. Take a piece of scrap paper and write down these numbers. Then we'll see if the books are on the shelf, and you can decide which one you want."

For the next hour or so, I was very, very busy. I helped kids find books, passed out reading lists, offered suggestions about which books to start with, and helped kids fill out registration forms. There were, as I had guessed, a lot of BSC clients at the library. Corrie's ten-year-old brother Sean was there, and so was Betsy Sobak, who's eight. Norman and Sarah Hill were also there. I saw the Hobart brothers and Haley Braddock.

Several Pike kids were there, of course: Nicky, Jordan, Byron, and Vanessa were busy picking out books. Actually, Jordan and Nicky were busier acting out a puppet show that had something to do with a gorilla that eats a town, and Vanessa was sitting in a corner with a poetry book (she plans to be a poet when she's older), but Byron was stacking up a bunch of books about reptiles. He adores snakes and other slithery things. "I can't *wait* to read these," he said. "It's so cool that I get certificates for something I want to do anyway!"

I was glad to see that Byron was excited about the Readathon, especially after I heard a few kids, including Nicky and Sean, complaining that their parents or teachers had pushed them into participating. I thought that was a shame. Kids should see reading as something fun, not as something they *have* to do.

I worked hard that afternoon, so hard I almost forgot about the BSC meeting until I glanced at my watch and realized I'd be late if I didn't run for it. What a change from the Monday before, when I had been watching the clock all afternoon, waiting for the meeting to start! I called a quick good-bye to Ms. Feld and Miss Ellway, and dashed out the door.

I arrived at the meeting in time, but I have to say I didn't pay much attention to anything that went on that day. I was too busy wondering what book might interest Sean Addison in reading and trying to remember whether Nicky had signed his registration form. I was already wrapped up in my new job.

I did tune in when Mrs. Wilder called, looking for someone to help Rosie with the Readathon. Rosie Wilder is a very busy seven-year-old: besides acting in commercials, she takes about eighteen different kinds of lessons — dancing and acting and singing and violin. Actually, she takes fewer lessons now than she used to; her parents decided not long ago that she was a little overloaded. But apparently *now* her parents had decided she could participate in the Readathon. However, they realized she'd need help signing up sponsors and so forth. They also wanted a sitter to take her to the library periodically, since they have such busy schedules. Kristy volunteered for the job, and she was the only one free, so she got it. We smiled at each other after she called Mrs. Wilder back. "This'll be great," I said. "I mean, working at the library is fun anyway, but having you there will make it even better."

Blues? What blues? I could hardly even remember why I had been feeling down the week before. The Readathon had cured me completely.

CHAPTER 4

"Protect the children!"

"No more filth!"

As I headed toward the library on Wednesday afternoon, I passed a small but very loud group of demonstrators. They stood on the library lawn, near the front entrance. Most of them were carrying signs which said things such as "What about family values?" and "Don't poison our children's minds!" As people walked to and from the library, the demonstrators shouted out their slogans.

I remembered the letter to the editor of the *Stoneybrook News* about book banning, and figured it must have been sent by this group. I hadn't paid much attention to it at the time, but now I could hardly ignore what they were saying.

I have never understood why people want to ban books. I mean, if *they* don't want to read certain books, that's fine. And I guess what they let their own children read is up to them, too. But why should they keep other people from reading what they choose? My dad has never stopped me from reading anything I wanted to, and I don't feel that *my* mind has been poisoned. True, some books have bad words in them, but so what? It isn't as though I would never hear those words anywhere else. And reading those books doesn't make me want to use the words myself. As for books that are about subjects such as divorce or drugs, well, those things exist in the world, and books aren't the *cause*.

I remember our school librarian once talked to us about books that have been banned from schools and libraries in this country. Some really terrific books are among them: *To Kill a Mockingbird*, *The Diary of Anne Frank*, and *The Outsiders*, to name a few. Some people think they're dangerous. For instance, *The Outsiders* was banned partly because a lot of the characters in the book came from "broken homes." Well, I have a lot of friends from "broken homes" — Kristy, Dawn, and Stacey, for example — and they're all good people. Good people who might really learn something from reading about *other* kids whose parents are divorced.

If I'd had time, I might have stopped to talk to the demonstrators, so I could try to understand why they were doing what they were doing. They didn't look like bad people, and obviously they believed in their cause. I would have been interested to hear what they had to say. But I didn't want to be late for my job, so I walked past them and went on into the library.

The children's room was packed with kids. The noise level was pretty high, but I could hear the demonstrators outside, even over the sound of all those kids talking and giggling. "Did you see those people out there?" I asked Ms. Feld, as I stopped at the main desk to pick up a batch of registration forms.

She nodded. "They have a right to demonstrate," she said. "Freedom of speech and all that. But I wish they would just come in and talk to me. I have to go through a certain process whenever people have a problem with a particular book, and I would be glad to explain it to them. As a librarian I don't believe in banning books, but I do feel that everyone has a right to voice his concerns." She picked up a flier from the desk and showed it to me. "This is the list of books they want to ban," she said. "They were handing these fliers out."

I glanced at the list, but I didn't have time to read it carefully. I noticed that *To Kill a Mockingbird* was on it, but before I could check out the other titles I felt a tug on my sleeve. I looked down to see Nicky Pike smiling up at me.

"Hi, Mary Anne," he said. "Can you help me find a book to read?"

"Sure," I replied. "See you later," I told Ms. Feld. I grabbed a third-grade reading list and ran my finger down it. "How about this one, Nicky?" I asked, pointing to a book about robots.

"Okay," he said, unenthusiastically. "I guess so."

I led Nicky to the card catalog, gave him a quick lesson in how to use it, then brought him to the shelf to find the book. He looked a little more interested when he saw the cover of the book, which featured a robot that could mow the lawn. "Awesome! Thanks, Mary Anne," he added, as he settled into a nearby corner with the book.

I looked around to see who else was at the library that afternoon. Many of the kids who had been there on Monday were back, plus some others. I saw plenty of kids I didn't recognize, but there were also quite a few I knew well.

Haley Braddock was sitting near the Raggedy Ann doll, reading intently and twirling a strand of the doll's yarn hair around her finger. Sean Addison was clowning around near the puppet theatre with a few other boys. I saw Marilyn and Carolyn Arnold, a pair of identical twins we sit for, looking over the new fiction, and Corrie Addison sitting at a table, reading her mummy book.

A boy I didn't know asked for help with his registration form, and he and I sat down at one of the tables to work on it. Just as we were finishing, I felt a tap on my shoulder. There stood Kristy, with Rosie Wilder in tow. "You look busy," she said.

"I *am*. Isn't it great?" I asked, looking around at the room full of children. "All these kids are so excited about reading." Then I saw a couple of girls scattering puzzle pieces on the floor. "Well, maybe not *all* of them," I added, smiling.

"Can we start finding books now?" asked Rosie. "I want to take home a whole bunch of them." Her glasses had slipped down her nose, and she pushed them up with her forefinger. Rosie is a very pretty little girl, with thick red hair, tons of freckles, and hazel eyes.

"Sure," said Kristy. "But maybe we ought to fill out one of these registration forms first." She and Rosie sat down with me at the table, and I showed them how to fill out the form.

"I bet I can win that prize," said Rosie. "I love to read. Last week I read six Boxcar Children books!"

"That's terrific," I replied. "There are some other kids here who read a lot, too. Maybe you'd like to meet them, and talk about books together." Sometimes I worry that Rosie is so busy with her lessons that she doesn't have as many friends as she could. "In fact, here comes one now." I had seen Charlotte Johanssen arrive, and now I waved her over. "Do you know Charlotte?" I asked Rosie. "You two are in the same grade at school, so maybe you've met."

Charlotte is a quiet, sweet, and very smart eight-year-old. She smiled at Rosie. "You're Rosie Wilder, right?" she asked. "I've seen you in that pudding commercial on TV."

"I know who you are, too," said Rosie. "I heard the special book report you gave about the Narnia series, in assembly that day." They grinned at each other and sat down to look over their reading lists and decide where to start. Charlotte checked off about nineteen books, and then asked me to help her collect them. I had just started to tell her that maybe it would be fairer to the other kids if she took only three or four books at a time, when suddenly the fire alarm began to ring — *loudly*. I gasped and looked around. So many kids were in that room! Frantically, I tried to think about the best way to get them all out of the building without anybody panicking.

Ms. Feld and Miss Ellway called Kristy and me over, and the four of us began lining the kids up by the exit doors. The children were surprisingly calm, although I did hear a few sniffles from the younger ones, some of whom looked pretty scared.

Kristy leaned over and whispered in my ear, "Do you smell smoke?" Her eyes were wide.

I sniffed and nodded. This was no fire drill. This was for real! I drew in a deep breath and told myself to stay calm. I couldn't lose my head as long as I was partly responsible for making sure the kids left the building safely.

Then I heard footsteps in the hall, and Mrs. Kishi burst into the room. "It's all right!" she said. She was a bit out of breath, but she seemed fairly calm. "We had a little fire, but we found it and it's already out. Nothing to worry about."

Within minutes, the kids had returned to what they had been doing, and the noise level in the children's room had returned to normal. Kristy and I looked at each other. "Close one," she said. I nodded. It took awhile for my heart to stop racing, but once it did I put the fire behind me and enjoyed the rest of my afternoon at the library.

Later that evening, at our BSC meeting, Claudia told us that she'd heard about the fire. "Mom called after it was over," she said. "She told me it was only a little fire, but that it was kind of scary at first, before they found it."

"Where was it?" I asked. "Kristy and I both smelled smoke. It must have been downstairs somewhere."

"It was," said Claud. "You know where the bathrooms are, in that hall outside the main children's room? The fire was in a sink in one of the bathrooms."

There are three bathrooms: one for men (and boys), one for women (and girls), and one for staff. Two doors lead into that hall from the children's room. "Mom thinks it was just a prank," Claud continued. "Some kid probably did it on a bet or something."

"Well, it was a dumb thing to do," I said. "It scared me to death. A *lot* of kids were in the library. Plus, what if the books caught on fire? That would be awful!"

Pretty soon the phone started to ring, and we forgot about the fire and got down to business. The Readathon was turning into a big plus for the BSC; lots of parents were calling on us to take their kids to the library in the afternoons.

When I returned home that night, I called Dawn. We hadn't talked in awhile, and I was eager to tell her about my job at the library. We spent a long time on the phone, catching up on each other's news.

I filled Dawn in on the Readathon, and the excitement over the fire at the library. Dawn told me about one of the kids she's been sitting for in California. She belongs to a baby-sitters club out there, too. It's called the We ♥ Kids Club, and while it's not as businesslike as our club, the members are good, enthusiastic sitters.

It was great to hear Dawn's voice. After I hung up, I realized that even though I didn't have the blues anymore, I missed her like crazy. I missed Logan, too. And Mallory. But you know what I *didn't* miss? I didn't miss moping around, thinking about how much I miss people!

CHAPTER 5

Wednesday,

I'm not even going to write about what happened at the library this afternoon, because I know it's the first thing we'll talk about at our meeting. Instead, I'll explain how I found out sort of a secret about Rosie Wilder today. It shouldn't have been surprising, but it was. I always thought Rosie was so self-assured and outgoing, but the fact is that she has a shy streak. It all started when I arrived at her house this afternoon.

Kristy was sitting for Rosie. It was a week after the fire at the library. And that day, she discovered something. While Rosie was having no trouble zooming through a pile of books for the Readathon, she wasn't exactly leading the race for sponsors. Rosie's sign-up sheet was almost blank, except for the names of her mother, her father, and her grandmother.

"It's too bad you don't have more sponsors," said Kristy, looking at the sheet. "You could make a lot of money for the library, and they really need it."

"I just want to read the books," said Rosie. "I don't want to have to ask people to sponsor me."

"There's nothing to it," said Kristy. "I'm sure people would be glad to sponsor you."

"But I don't know how to ask them. I mean, if this was a telethon or something, and I could sing and dance for the cameras, that would be no problem. But I don't want to knock on people's doors and talk to them in person."

Kristy nodded. She thought she understood Rosie's problem. As a child actress, Rosie was used to dealing with people — especially grown-ups — *as* an actress, not as herself. If she couldn't be in character, she wasn't sure how to relate. Kristy thought for a second, and an idea flashed into her mind. "Tell you what,

Rosie," she said. "You have to practice for your dance lesson, right? Why don't you get started on that, and when you're done I'll have something to show you."

Kristy and Rosie headed down to the Wilders' basement, where Rosie has a ballet *barre* on a mirrored wall. Kristy sat in a corner with a clipboard on her lap, writing, while Rosie rehearsed a routine she was working on. Her music was a little distracting, but Kristy tried hard to concentrate on what she was writing. "You are the one," blared the singer, "my moon and sun." Rosie spun around the studio, frowning slightly as she worked to remember her routine. "I have to remind myself how young she is sometimes," said Kristy. (I think a lot of people do.) Despite her talent, she's just a little kid.

When she had finished practicing, Rosie collapsed next to Kristy. "What are you writing?" she asked.

Kristy smiled. "It's a script. All you have to do is memorize these lines. It'll work like a charm."

Rosie took her glasses from the shelf where she'd left them, and began to read out loud. "Hello, Mr. Blank, my name is Rosie Wilder," she said. She began to giggle. "Mr. Blank?"

"That's where you put in the person's name," Kristy said. "We'll go door-to-door in your neighborhood, so you'll already know everybody's name."

Rosie nodded and went back to the script. "I'm your neighbor," she read. "And I'm here to ask you to be my sponsor in a Readathon to raise funds for the children's room at the Stoneybrook Library. Smile."

"The smile is a stage direction," said Kristy, gently. "You're not supposed to *say* that, just do it."

Rosie giggled again. "Stage directions are always in parentheses," she told Kristy. "Like when they say, 'Exit, stage right.' It's in parentheses, so you know not to say it."

"Oh, right!" said Kristy. "I should have remembered that from reading plays in English class. Okay, let's fix that." She took the clipboard and went over the script, adding a few marks. Then she handed it back to Rosie. "So, what do you think?"

"It's a great idea," said Rosie, when she had finished reading. "But the script is a little — well, it's a little boring." She glanced at Kristy as if to make sure she wasn't hurting her feelings. "Do you mind if I fix it up a little?"

"Be my guest," said Kristy. She ran upstairs to fix a snack, leaving Rosie bent over the clipboard, scribbling away. Half an hour later, she and Rosie headed out. Rosie had changed into a sailor dress and tied a blue ribbon in her hair.

They walked over to the house next door, and Kristy rang the bell. Rosie whipped off her glasses and handed them to Kristy. "Hold these, okay?" she whispered. Then she licked her lips and pinched her cheeks to make them pink. She seemed to gather herself together as footsteps sounded from the hall inside the house. When the door swung open, Rosie was standing tall and wearing a charming smile. She went right into her script, and Kristy watched, amazed. She told me later that Rosie was so professional and so persuasive that there was no way any of the neighbors could resist her.

They went from house to house, and the sign-up sheet filled up fast. Along the way, Rosie added to the "script" until it was as polished as a TV commercial. "This is great," she told Kristy. "All I have to do is pretend I'm auditioning for a part. The part of Rosie Wilder, a little girl who's in a Readathon!"

Kristy laughed. "I'd definitely give you the part," she said. "Hey, it looks like Rosie's sheet is full. Should we head for the library?"

"Sure," replied Rosie. "After I stop at home and change my clothes. This sailor dress is itchy."

A little while later, Rosie (dressed in jeans and a T-shirt) looked like a regular kid again. On the way to the library, she carried her full sign-up sheet proudly. "Wait till Ms. Feld sees *this*," she said. "And I'm going to pick out eight more books today. That will bring my total to fifteen for one week!"

"All right!" Kristy held up her hand for a high-five, and Rosie smacked it. They walked into the children's room together. "Hey, Mary Anne," said Kristy, when she saw me. "What are you doing way over there in that corner?" Rosie headed for the bookshelves, and Kristy came to my corner to talk to me.

"I'm looking for a book," I said. Then I added something in a whisper.

"What?" asked Kristy. "You're trying to play a game with fizzy Del Rey?"

"Shh!" I hissed. I repeated what I had said, whispering again.

"Oh!" said Kristy, nodding. "You're trying to stay away from Miss Ellway. I don't blame you. She seems like a real meanie."

I did not like Miss Ellway too much, and whenever I worked in the children's room I made a point of staying out of her way. If she was at the main desk, I worked at the card catalog. If she was at the card catalog, I stayed in the games-and-puzzles corner. If she decided to straighten up the puzzles, I would head for the biography section. Of course, all this time I was giving help to any kids who needed it. I wasn't dodging the *kids* — just Miss Ellway.

"Kristy!" Rosie was tugging on Kristy's sleeve. "I can't find the books I was looking for."

"Maybe we can help you," I said. "What books do you want to find?"

"The ones about a magic school bus," said Rosie. "I saw them in school, and they were awesome."

"Let's check the card catalog," I said, leading her over to it. I pulled out a drawer, and then I almost dropped it on my foot. Why? Because the fire alarm began to ring.

"Oh, my lord!" said Kristy. "Not again." She sniffed, and I did too. There was definitely smoke in the air.

"I don't believe it." I looked around the room. Once again, the place was full of kids. And once again, it took everything I had to keep from panicking. Ms. Feld and Miss Ellway jumped from behind their desks and began lining the kids up, and Kristy and I helped to gather the kids who were scattered throughout the room. I kept expecting Mrs. Kishi to come in, the way she had the week before, and tell us everything was fine.

She came in, all right, but not to tell us that

things were okay. Instead, she began to help Ms. Feld. As she gently guided a few stray kids into line, she spoke to Ms. Feld in a low voice. Kristy and I edged closer to her, hoping to catch what she was saying. " — fire department is on its way," we heard. "They'll be here any second, but we need to get everyone out of the building. This fire isn't as small as the other one." She looked very serious. Her face was pale, and her voice was strained.

Luckily, evacuating the kids went smoothly. It was almost as if last week's fire had been a dress rehearsal for this one. The kids behaved incredibly well, and we had moved them out of the building within minutes. I noticed that Rosie was gripping Kristy's hand tightly. A small group of kids was sticking close to Kristy and me — all kids we sit for often. Nicky was there, and Charlotte, and Norman Hill. They looked pretty scared.

At least until the fire engines pulled up, sirens wailing. "Awesome!" shouted Nicky, watching the first fire fighters jump off the truck and run into the building. The kids seemed to forget their fear as they took in every detail of what the fire fighters were wearing, what they carried, and how they attached their hoses to the fire hydrant on the sidewalk near the front entrance of the library.

"This is so cool," said Rosie.

Kristy and I exchanged glances. We didn't think it was cool at all, but it was better not to let the kids focus on how awful a fire in the library could be. We agreed, without speaking (best friends can do that, you know), not to say a word to the kids.

It didn't take the fire fighters long to put out the fire — in fact, they never even had to use the hose they had hooked up. Hand-held fire extinguishers seemed to be enough. Soon Kristy and I and the kids had returned to the children's room. I was helping Rosie find those books she had wanted, while Kristy stayed in the office area, talking with Ms. Feld and Mrs. Kishi, who were discussing the fire.

Kristy and I walked Rosie home that afternoon, and then she and I headed to Claudia's for the BSC meeting. Along the way, she told me what Mrs. Kishi had said. "It was a bigger fire than the other one," she told me, "mainly because it was started with lighter fluid. It was in a garbage can outside the back door of the children's room. You know, the door that hardly anybody uses? The one that leads to the back hallway? We're lucky it didn't spread."

"We sure are. Is Mrs. Kishi worried?"

Kristy nodded. "That part about the lighter fluid scared her. She thinks somebody's getting serious about these fires."

"I just can't believe it," I said. "Who on earth would want to burn down a library?"

"I don't know, but I think we need to find out."

We had a mystery on our hands, and it was time to start solving it — before the town of Stoneybrook lost its library.

CHAPTER 6

Kristy was right when she'd written in the club notebook that the fire in the library was the first thing we talked about at our meeting. In fact, it was the *only* thing. Usually Kristy likes to focus on club business, at least at the beginning of each meeting, but on Wednesday she seemed to forget that rule.

She and I arrived at Claudia's just before five-thirty. We were both out of breath, and we were still a little freaked out by what had happened at the library. Kristy took a few minutes to scribble some notes about her job with Rosie, and by the time she was done the other club members had arrived. Then Kristy called the meeting to order, but we skipped over the club business and started talking about the fire.

Kristy was sitting in the director's chair, of course. Shannon sat next to Claudia and me on the bed, and Stacey sat on the floor, leaning against Claud's bureau. Jessi sat on the floor, too, but she wasn't leaning. As usual, she was using the time to keep her legs limber with a series of painful-looking ballet stretches.

Claudia passed around some Reese's peanut butter cups — and handed Stacey a box of pretzels — while Kristy and I told our friends the news. I know we sounded upset.

"I don't feel *responsible*," I said, thinking out loud. "But I *do* feel involved. I mean, there have been two fires since I started working at the library."

"I feel involved, too," said Kristy. "I was there for both fires, and I can't think of any clues or remember anybody acting suspicious, or anything. It seems like we should have more to go on than we do."

"I just can't believe someone would want to burn down the library," said Jessi. She was bent over, with her face nearly touching the floor between her outspread legs, so her voice was a little muffled. I could tell she was upset, too, though.

"Me, neither," said Shannon. "What a crazy thing to do."

"That's what worries *me*," said Claudia. "Whoever is setting the fires must be kind of a nut or something. Plus, I'm worried about my mom. After all, she's in that building all day, every day. A library seems like such a safe place. I've never even *thought* about her being in danger before. But now I think about it all the time."

I patted Claudia on the back. "She'll be okay," I said. "She knows how to deal with emergencies. You should have seen how calm she was today."

"What about the kids, though?" asked Stacey. "I mean, you can't expect that *kids* will always stay calm during emergencies. It sounds like they did well the first couple of times, but who knows what might happen if that alarm rings again?"

So there we sat, a whole room full of worrywarts. "Well, I guess the question is," said Kristy, "what are we going to do about it?"

Everyone was silent for a minute. "What *can* we do?" asked Shannon, finally.

"We have to catch the firebug," I said firmly. The words popped out of my mouth, surprising me as much as everyone else. But as soon as I said them, I knew they were true. I wasn't going to rest easy until the person setting the fires had been caught. And why couldn't *we* be the ones to catch him (or her)?

"You're right," said Kristy.

"I still can't imagine *who* would want to burn down the library," said Jessi. Now she was in this really weird position, kind of standing on her shoulders, with her legs back over her head. Her voice sounded like Donald Duck's.

"*What* are you doing, Jessi?" asked Stacey. "That looks incredibly uncomfortable."

"It's a yoga position," said Jessi, as she brought her legs back down to earth and sat up. "It's called the Plow. It's great for your circulation. Anyway, I think the thing to do is to try to imagine *who* might want to burn down the library."

Once again, silence filled the room. Then the phone rang, startling us a little. Kristy answered it, a bit distractedly. The caller was Mrs. Pike, looking for a sitter who could go to the library with Nicky occasionally, since he needed a little extra Readathon help. Jessi volunteered. "Picking him up will give me a chance to spend some time with Mal," she said.

"Hey!" shouted Claudia, all of a sudden.

I nearly fell off the bed. "What?" I asked, as soon as I had recovered. "What is it, Claud?"

"I just remembered something my mom once told me. You guys are *not* going to believe this." She looked at each of us in turn, her eyes gleaming.

"What? *What?*" asked Kristy. "Just *tell* us, already!"

"Okay," Claudia began, in a hushed voice. "See, the library is built on land that used to belong to a really rich family. It was a huge estate, but over time the family lost money and had to sell off some of the land. At the same time, they donated this one piece of land to the town of Stoneybrook, with the understanding that the town would build a library on it."

"Claudia," said Kristy, with a warning tone in her voice. "Is there a point to this story?"

"Absolutely," said Claudia, holding up a hand. "Just give me a second here. See, the family donated the land, but there were strings attached. They donated it under one condition: that if the library that was built on the property was ever torn down or destroyed, the land would go back to the family."

"We're still *wait*ing," said Kristy, in a singsong voice. "What are you getting at?"

"I'm getting at this," replied Claudia, leaning forward. "The family who donated the land? Their name was Ellway."

I gasped. "You mean — "

Claudia nodded. "Miss Ellway, who's working in the children's room. It was her grandfather who gave — or was it lent? — the land to Stoneybrook."

"But if she's so rich," I said, "why is she working as an aide in the children's room?"

"She isn't so rich. The Ellways have been losing money, remember? She's facing hard times, so she had to take a job."

"This is incredible!" said Kristy. "Are you saying what I *think* you're saying, Claud?"

"I'm saying that maybe Miss Ellway needs money really badly. Badly enough to consider burning down the library and reclaiming her family's land."

"Whoa!" I said. "That's a pretty serious accusation."

Claudia nodded. "I know. But think about it. Does Miss Ellway really seem to enjoy working with children? Or do you think she might just have taken that job so she could do her dirty work without being suspected?"

Claudia was excited about her theory. I wasn't so sure. I wasn't crazy about Miss Ellway, but to accuse her of trying to burn down the library seemed a little farfetched. "I don't know," I said. "I agree we should keep an eye on her, but there are other things we need to think about, too."

"Such as?" asked Kristy, raising an eyebrow. I think she was a little surprised to see me speaking up so much.

"Well, such as the fires themselves. I think the more we know about them, the better. Like, what *kind* of fire was that first one? What was burning in the sink?"

"Probably just paper towels or toilet paper

or something," said Stacey, "since it was in the bathroom."

"But do we know for sure?" I didn't know why I was pressing the point, but it seemed important.

"I can call my mom and ask," said Claudia. "I mean, I still think it was Miss Ellway, but you're probably right that the more we know, the better." She reached for the phone and called her mother at the library. "Mrs. Kishi, please," she said, and then waited until her mom picked up the phone. "Hi, Mom," she said. "We're having a club meeting, and we were talking about the fires, and we were just wondering — what was burning, anyway? Was it, like, paper towels or something?" She listened for a second, and her jaw dropped. "Wow, really?" she said. "That's kind of creepy."

"What? What?" we all asked. Claudia motioned for us to be quiet. "Why did we want to know?" she asked. "Oh, no reason. Just curious, I guess. Anyway, thanks! I'll let you get back to work. 'Bye." Claudia put down the phone. "I don't want her worrying that we're doing anything dangerous," she explained. "Listen to this! Guess what was burning?"

"*Claudia!*" said Kristy, with that warning tone in her voice again. "We don't *want* to guess. We're waiting for you to tell us."

"Okay, okay," said Claud. "Get this — it was a book! A paperback book."

Once again, there was total silence in the room. Well, maybe not *total* silence. I heard a few gasps.

"Okay," said Kristy, who was the first to recover. "This is getting really serious. That is just too weird to ignore — burning a book in a bathroom sink in the library. Now we really have to solve this mystery." She whipped the pencil out from behind her ear and began to make a list on a piece of scrap paper from Claudia's desk. "Number one," she said, as she wrote, "keep an eye on Miss Ellway."

"Definitely," Claudia agreed. "And I'll see if I can find out anything more about the deal with the land. Maybe there's something I forgot."

"Number two. Keep an eye on everybody else, too. Look for suspicious behavior, and keep a list of possible suspects," I suggested.

"Good," said Kristy.

"Number three," said Jessi. "Find out about the second fire, too. Claudia didn't ask what was burning *today*."

"Check," said Kristy, writing it down.

"Number four," said Shannon. "Try to prevent future fires."

"Oh, good one!" I exclaimed.

"And number five," said Stacey. "Solve this mystery before the library and all the books in it get burned to a crisp."

"All *right*!" said Kristy, scribbling away and then holding up the list. "We're ready for action. Watch out, Mr. — or Madame — Firebug. The BSC is on your case!"

CHAPTER 7

By the end of our meeting that Wednesday, we had agreed on a plan of action. The next afternoon, right after school, Kristy, Claudia, and I headed for the library together, hoping to turn up some clues. Jessi had a dance class, and Stacey and Shannon were baby-sitting, but the three of us had decided to get started.

Since Wednesday wasn't my regular day at the library, Ms. Feld looked surprised when I came in. "Mary Anne!" she said, smiling up at me. She was, as usual, doing three things at once: signing out a pile of books for a little girl, calculating overdue fines for a father who had returned books late, and helping a little boy fill out a library card. "I guess you just can't stay away, can you?" she said, not skipping a beat in her work.

"Um," I began, trying frantically to think of something to say to Ms. Feld — something that wouldn't include the words "scene of the crime," which Claudia had just whispered as we made our way down the stairs. She likes to use Nancy Drew terminology whenever she can.

"We're just passing through," said Kristy, giving me a little push. "See you!" She smiled and waved, and so did I. "No sense in getting caught up in conversation," Kristy whispered to me as we hurried through the door and into the hallway where the bathrooms are.

Claudia tried the door on the women's room. "Darn, it's locked," she said. "I forgot. My mom said they decided to start locking the bathrooms after the fire. They keep the keys at the main desk, upstairs. You have to ask for one if you want to use the bathroom."

"Doesn't Ms. Feld have one, too?" I asked.

"She must," said Claudia. "Let's ask her. And I'll try to get the staff bathroom key, too. After all, we don't even know which bathroom the fire was *in*. I never thought of asking."

We trooped back into the children's room. "Excuse me, but do you have the bathroom key?" Kristy asked Miss Ellway, who had taken over for Ms. Feld at the checkout desk. Miss Ellway gave a little sigh and bent to rustle through a drawer.

"Here it is," she said. "Now don't go locking it in the bathroom, or you'll have to go upstairs to get the other one for me. I don't have time to be chasing around for keys."

Kristy thanked Miss Ellway politely, but when she turned around to face me, she squinched up her eyes and wrinkled her nose, and I bit my tongue trying to keep from laughing. *Why* did Miss Ellway have to be such a sourpuss?

Claudia, meanwhile, had gone to Ms. Feld's office area to ask her for the staff bathroom key. "Well, Claudia," I heard Ms. Feld say, "officially that bathroom is for staff use only, but I guess since it's an emergency, staff *daughters* are okay, too." She grinned at Claudia, who was blushing a little, and handed her the key.

"What did you *say* to her?" I whispered, as we returned to the hall.

Claudia giggled. "I just said I didn't think I'd make it if I had to wait for both of you to use the bathroom before I had a turn," she said.

"*Claudia!*" I was *so* embarrassed. I wouldn't say a thing like that if you paid me a million dollars.

"Unfortunately, I couldn't think of any reason to ask for the *boys'* room key," Claudia went on. "We'll just have to inspect the other two now, and maybe Logan can stop by and check the men's room tomorrow."

"I'll ask him," I said.

Kristy was opening the door to the women's room and now the three of us stepped inside. The bathroom was clean and neat, and the sink showed no signs of a fire. We looked around for a second, but there was really nothing to see, so we left, making sure the door was locked behind us, and Claudia unlocked the staff bathroom.

We checked out the sink, and the stalls, too — just for good measure.

"Looks fine," Claudia said. "I don't think there was any fire in here, either."

After we checked the bathrooms, we decided to look at the other "scene of the crime," by the back door. But the trash can had apparently been moved already, so there wasn't much to see.

"Now what?" I said.

"We better take the keys back, first of all," said Claudia. "Then we can go upstairs and talk to my mom. Maybe she can tell us a little more about the fires."

We returned the keys, with thanks to Miss Ellway and Ms. Feld. "See you tomorrow," I said to Ms. Feld. Then we headed upstairs.

Mrs. Kishi was at her desk, working with a calculator. "Hi, Mom," said Claudia.

"Just a second," replied Mrs. Kishi, holding up one hand. She punched in a few more numbers, wrote something down, and leaned back in her chair. "I *hate* making budgets," she said, smiling. "How are you girls?"

"Fine," said Claudia. "We're just looking around. We were trying to find out more about those fires, as a matter of fact."

"Oh, the fires," said Mrs. Kishi, frowning. "I just hope there aren't any more."

"Me, too," I said. "By the way, do you know what book was burned in that first fire?" I was curious.

Mrs. Kishi shrugged. "That's a good question. I assume it was a library book, so I *will* have to replace it, but the fire department didn't say."

We talked to Mrs. Kishi for a few minutes more, but we didn't find out much. Then the three of us headed back to Claudia's house, feeling discouraged. "We need some clues," said Kristy, plopping down in the director's chair.

"I have an idea," I said. It had come to me as we walked to Claudia's. I picked up the phone. I don't know what gave me the courage to do what I did next, but somehow I managed. I dialed the fire department and sat back, waiting for someone to pick up.

"What are you doing?" asked Claudia.

"Shh!" I said. "Hello?" I put on my most

adult voice. "I'm calling for Mrs. Kishi, at the Stoneybrook Public Library. . . . About the fires." The person who had answered the phone put me on hold, and as I waited I could feel my heart beating hard. "Hello," I said, when a man identifying himself as Lieutenant Joffrey picked up the phone. "I'm calling for Mrs. Kishi. She wondered if it might be possible to find out the name of the book that was burned in the bathroom. If it was a library book I need to know the title, so we can replace it." I heard Lieutenant Joffrey ask someone else a quick question, and then he got back on the line.

"It was Beanie, or something like that. The author was Judy Blume," he said. "And it was definitely from your library. Only the front was burned, and there was one of those little pockets in the back."

"*Deenie!*" I said, forgetting to sound adult. I knew that book, and I liked it.

"There was a library book in the trash can, too," said Lieutenant Joffrey, before I could figure out what I was going to say next. "You know, the second fire. You'll probably want to replace that one, too, won't you?"

"Oh — right!" I said. I was so surprised to hear that *another* book had been burned that I almost forgot the story I had made up about why I was calling. "And what was the title of that one?"

He paused for a second, as if he were checking his notes. *"A Light in the Attic,"* he replied. "Funny title. Anyway, it's by somebody named Silverstein. Shel Silverstein."

"Wow," I said. Somebody was picking some good books to burn. I like the poems in *A Light in the Attic*. Then I realized I wasn't sounding very official, so I said, "Thank you very much, sir. You've been very helpful."

"You're welcome," he said, sounding bewildered. I think I had changed my voice on him about five times.

I hung up the phone and turned to Claudia and Kristy. "You guys are not going to believe this," I began. "A book was burned in the other fire, too."

"We figured that out," said Kristy impatiently. "What books did they burn?"

I told them.

"I don't get it," said Kristy. "Why would anyone set books on fire?"

"What else is there to burn in a library?" asked Claudia, with a shrug.

She had a point. But then I thought of something. "You know, I don't think this is something Miss Ellway would bother with," I said. "If somebody was determined to destroy the library — I mean, burn the whole thing down

— why would she make little fires in places like sinks and trash cans?"

Kristy was looking at me and nodding. "You're right," she said. "If you really wanted to burn a place down, you'd just pour gasoline all over the floor and run for it."

"Yuck," said Claudia. We sat quietly for a moment, imagining the library in flames. It was a horrible thing even to think about. Then Kristy looked at her watch.

"I have to get going," she said. "I'm meeting Charlie over at the high school, and he's going to give me a ride home."

"I'll walk with you," I said. "I should get home, too." I think we all felt a little overwhelmed. Now that we knew that not one, but *two* books had been burned, the fires at the library seemed more serious.

The next day, something happened that upset me. I was at the library, working with the Readathon kids. Things were quieting down a little, now that most of the kids were registered and their sponsors were lined up. I was still busy making reading suggestions and helping them find books, though. Anyway, what happened was this: I was looking with Nicky Pike for a book about dog-training. (The Pikes recently inherited a bassett hound from the Barretts.) I pulled it off the shelf for him, and we sat down at a table to look it over. As he was reaching for it, he knocked his jacket off his chair, and something fell out of his jacket pocket. Guess what it was.

A pack of matches. Matches with a red-and-white logo on them, the kind you see everywhere.

"Nicky!" I said, picking them up.

"What?" he asked, in this completely innocent voice. I showed him the matches, and he turned pale. "Those aren't mine," he said quickly.

"They were in your pocket," I replied gently. Something in his voice made me want to believe he was telling the truth.

"I don't know how they got there, I swear!" Nicky looked as if he were about to cry. I gave him a little hug.

"It's okay, Nicky," I said. "I believe you." I *did* believe him, too. But I couldn't help wondering how those matches had ended up in his pocket. This was serious business, and I knew I would have to bring it up at the club meeting.

Later on, when I did, we agreed that Nicky seemed to be telling the truth, and we decided not to tell Mr. and Mrs. Pike about the incident. We did call Mallory, though, and she talked for a long time with Nicky. He stuck to his story, insisting that he had not seen the matches before. He also insisted on helping us solve the mystery of the fires. He was determined to prove his innocence. It looked as if the BSC Detective Agency was going to have a new junior member.

CHAPTER 8

Monday

Ooh, la la. Spending the afternoon at a fancy French restaurant was <u>not</u> what I expected to be doing today, but that's how things worked out. No, I didn't eat any snails, and no, I didn't order champagne. So what <u>was</u> I doing there? Well, it's a long story.

After school on Monday, Jessi headed for the Pikes' house to pick up Nicky and take him to the library. She stopped at home first, so by the time she reached the Pikes' all the younger kids had returned home and the Pike household was in a state of chaos.

Vanessa answered the door. "Hi, Jessi," she said. "Want to hear the haiku I just wrote about wintertime?"

Before Jessi could answer, she heard a thundering sound as the triplets ran down the stairs. "Jessi!" said Adam. "We're having races upstairs! Want to come watch us?"

Then Claire traipsed into the room, looking elegant in a floor-length gown (actually one of Mrs. Pike's bathrobes) and high heels. "Lovely to meet you," she said. "I'm Mrs. Filthy-Rich, and I'd like to invite you to my tea party." Claire's five years old, and she adores dressing up.

"*Our* tea party," said Margo from behind her. Margo, who's seven, was dressed in a long white nightshirt that must have belonged to her father, and a pink feather boa.

"Know what, guys?" Jessi said. "I'd love to hear your poems and watch your races and drink tea with you, but I'm really just here to pick up Nicky."

"Nicky's in his room," said Adam. "We'll

get him." The triplets took off, thundering back up the stairs.

"And Mal's in the living room," said Vanessa.

"Lying down already," said Margo. "I guess school really tired her out today."

"She's no fun anymore," said Claire. "She can't do *anything*."

"She'll be better soon," said Jessi. "I bet she'll be playing with you again before you know it." She headed for the living room, and found Mal lying on the couch, a blanket covering her.

"Jessi!" said Mal. "Boy, is it great to see you. I feel like I never get to talk to you anymore, since I only see you at school." A huge stack of books sat next to the couch, plus a drawing pad, pens, and a tray with a bottle of ginger ale standing next to a glass. "Whatever you do," said Mal, "don't get mono. It's no fun."

"I know," said Jessi sympathetically. "You must be so tired of being sick."

"How's the BSC?" asked Mal. "Has everybody forgotten about me?"

"No way. Everybody misses you like crazy. Especially me." She handed Mallory a book she had brought. "I guess you're probably tired of reading, but I found this at the library, and I knew you'd like it. It's a new Marguerite Henry book, about this pony that's a descendant of Misty. The school library doesn't have it yet."

"Wow!" exclaimed Mal. "This looks terrific. Thanks a lot." She reached down and picked up the drawing pad. "I wanted to show you something," she said to Jessi. "I've been working on this idea for a picture book."

"Cool," said Jessi. "Let's see." But just then, Nicky ran into the room.

"Do we *have* to go the the library?" he asked Jessi. "I'd rather be in races."

"What about the Readathon, Nicky?" asked Jessi. "You already have your sponsors signed up and everything."

"I don't want to go to that dumb old library," muttered Nicky.

Jessi and Mal exchanged a Look. They both knew what was wrong with Nicky. Even though they believed what he had said about the matches, they knew he probably felt he was under suspicion. And, as Jessi told me later, she hated to think that Nicky might develop negative feelings for the library. He wasn't crazy about reading as it was.

"Come on, Nicky," said Jessi. "It'll be fun."

"Nicky, would you do me a favor and pick out a book for me while you're there?" asked Mallory. "That would be a big help."

"Oh, okay," said Nicky, kicking his toe into the couch. "But I still don't want to go."

"Didn't I hear that you wanted to help solve the mystery of the fires?" asked Jessi gently. "Maybe we could find some clues at the library."

Nicky's face brightened. "Do you think so? Okay, let's go!"

Jessi looked at Mal and shrugged. "I guess I'll look at your picture book idea next time," she said. She knew Mal would understand.

When Jessi and Nicky arrived at the library, they found the place mobbed. Along with everyone else, I was there, and so was Kristy, who was with Rosie. Jessi at first tried to interest Nicky in finding some books, but he seemed distracted. He walked around with her as she hunted through the shelves, but he obviously wasn't paying much attention. "Okay," said Jessi, finally. "I've found you two more books. How about if we sign them out, and maybe you can tell Ms. Feld about the book you just read. If you pass her quiz, she'll give you a certificate."

"Okay." Nicky followed Jessi to the main desk, and gave his name to Miss Ellway, who checked out the books for him. Then they found Ms. Feld, who was busy cutting up construction paper for a bulletin board display.

"Hi, Nicky," she said. "Did you want to tell me about a book you read?"

"Umm," said Nicky, looking down at his feet.

"What was it about?" asked Ms. Feld gently.

"Robots," said Nicky.

"Can you tell me a little more? For instance, what was one of the special robots they talked about in that book?"

"Umm," said Nicky. "I forget." His gaze was wandering all over the library, and Jessi could tell his mind was more on fires than robots.

"Maybe we'll try again tomorrow," said Jessi, smiling at Ms. Feld. "Okay, Nicky?"

Nicky nodded. As they left Ms. Feld's desk, He looked up at Jessi. "I can't think about that book until I find out who started those fires."

"I know," said Jessi sympathetically. She led Nicky to Kristy and Rosie who were reading near the Raggedy Ann doll. "Hi, you guys," she said, sitting down next to Kristy. "What's up?"

"We're just reading," said Kristy. "But I don't think Rosie has her mind on her book. She's been talking about the fires all afternoon."

"I think it's terrible," said Rosie. "I can't believe anybody would start a fire in a library. Especially *our* library. I want to find out who did it."

"Me, too!" said Nicky, excitedly. He turned to Jessi. "Can we be detectives now?" he asked.

Jessi looked at Kristy, and they shrugged. Apparently the kids didn't want to do anything else. Besides, they were pretty interested in the mystery themselves. "All right," said Jessi. "But I doubt we'll find much."

"I'm going to check out every corner of these rooms," said Nicky.

"Me, too," agreed Rosie. The two of them set off, with Kristy and Jessi following them. They poked around in back of the card catalog. They pulled books out of the shelves and peered behind them. They searched through the magazine rack. But they didn't turn up any clues.

"Where was that second fire, again?" asked Nicky.

"In a trash can," Jessi told him. "Just outside the back door."

"Let's look out there," said Nicky. He led the way. Since the trash can was gone, there wasn't much to see.

Rosie looked disappointed, but Nicky still looked determined. He went back into the children's room, leading the others, and turned his attention to the area around the back door. He moved a stool away from the wall and climbed it to check out the higher shelves. Rosie was looking at the lower ones. After a couple of minutes, Nicky stepped down from the stool and started to move it back to its original place.

"Hey," he said suddenly. He bent down and picked something up. "Look at this! It was under one of the stool's legs." He held out his hand, and we clustered around to take a look.

Jessi gasped. "It's a pack of matches!"

"Whoa," said Kristy. "I don't believe it. I bet these are the ones somebody used to set that fire."

"There's a few missing," said Rosie, who had opened the pack for a closer look.

"And the best part," said Nicky, "is that they're *not* the same kind of matches that were in my jacket pocket."

He was right. This one had a shiny cover. Jessi turned it over and saw "Chez Maurice" in gold script on the front. "These are from that French restaurant downtown," she said. "Wow, you guys. This is a *great* clue."

"Yeah!" said Nicky. "Now all we have to do is stake out the place, and we're bound to see the person who started the fires. Can we go now?"

Once again, Jessi and Kristy looked at each other and shrugged. "Why not?" said Jessi.

Kristy checked her watch. "We have some time before we need to get the kids home and head for our meeting," she said. "Okay, let's go."

"Yea!" shouted Nicky and Rosie.

"Shh!" I said. "Don't forget, you're in a library."

Kristy and Jessi filled me in quickly on what they had found and where they were going. I was dying to go with them, but I had to stay and help with the Readathon. I was trying to find a book — *any* book — for Sean Addison. It was so hard to get him excited about the Readathon.

So, that's how Jessi and Kristy and Nicky and Rosie ended up spending the afternoon at a fancy French restaurant. Of course, there wasn't much to see at Chez Maurice (that name means "at Maurice's house" in French, in case you're wondering) on a Monday afternoon. Since the lunch hour was over, the maître d' was practically the only one there (the maître d' is sort of the king of the waiters). He was polishing silver, and he didn't seem to want to be bothered with questions about his clients. His name did *not* happen to be Maurice, but Jessi told me later that he acted as if he owned the place.

"He was totally unhelpful," she said. "And even though we spied for over an hour, we didn't see a thing. It was too early for people to be arriving for dinner."

Nicky and Rosie were disappointed, and so were Kristy and Jessi. They were worried, too. This wasn't just a game — it was serious business. If they didn't catch the firebug soon, the library could go up in smoke.

CHAPTER 9

On the way from school to the library two days later, I was thinking about how much I loved my new job. I felt involved in it, and, except for my worries about the fires, very happy. It was still cold and gray outside, and I still missed Logan and Dawn and Mallory, but I wasn't bored anymore. Helping with the Readathon was keeping me awfully busy. Even when I wasn't actually at the library, I often found myself thinking about the job, figuring out how Norman Hill could find more sponsors, wondering which book Charlotte might want to read next, or trying to come up with a book Sean could get excited about.

As I neared the library, I noticed that the demonstrators were outside again. I had thought (okay, I had *hoped*) they had given up on getting those books banned, but I guess the cold weather had just kept them away for awhile. Now they were back, and shouting as loudly as ever. "Protect our children!" they yelled. "Keep Stoneybrook clean!" A couple of them smiled at me as I hurried by: a woman in a bright green knit cap and a man carrying a sign that showed a book behind one of those red circles with a slash through it.

I smiled back. I didn't want to seem unfriendly, even though I didn't agree with what they stood for.

"You seem like a nice young lady," said the woman with the hat. "Maybe you'd like to take one of these lists and look it over. We have a petition you can sign, if you agree that these books are dangerous for the children of Stoneybrook."

I took the list and smiled again, but I didn't say anything. I would never sign a petition to ban books, but that didn't mean I had to be rude. I made my way through the group of demonstrators and went into the library, giving the list a quick glance. The last time I'd seen it, I'd only noticed *To Kill A Mockingbird*. This time, I spotted some titles that really surprised me: *Huckleberry Finn* was on the list, and so was *The Grapes of Wrath*. I always thought those books were classics. What could be wrong with them? I also saw *Bridge to Terabithia*, by Katherine Paterson, which is a book I *loved*. I couldn't remember anything terrible about it.

I shoved the list into my jacket pocket as I entered the children's room. A lot of kids were there already, and Ms. Feld and Miss Ellway both looked busy. Ms. Feld was simultaneously talking on the phone, repairing a ripped book jacket, and checking out a stack of cassettes for a harried-looking mother with a baby in her arms. Miss Ellway was at the checkout desk, where a line of four or five kids, including Sarah Hill and Byron Pike, waited to take out books. "Oh, Mary Anne," she said. "I'm glad to see you. These two boys here need some help finding books." She pointed at Nicky (who had apparently come with his brother that day) and another boy I didn't recognize. "I haven't had a moment to help them." She smiled at me, and suddenly I felt bad about judging her as quickly as I had. Maybe she just needed a little more time to warm up to people. She certainly seemed friendlier all of a sudden.

I smiled at her. "Okay," I said. I led the boys into the other room. Kristy was there, working with Rosie, but I just waved to her, since I knew we'd be able to talk later. I got right down to work. The boy I didn't recognize turned out to be named Matthew Bailey, and it was easy to find the book he wanted. Nicky was a different story. He didn't seem to have his mind on the Readathon. Instead of looking for books, he glanced longingly at the puppet theatre, where Sean and some other boys were playing.

"Nicky, are you sure you want to be in the Readathon?" I asked him, as I looked over his registration sheet. "You have a lot of sponsors signed up so far, but you've only read that one book about robots."

"I know," mumbled Nicky. "I just don't like any of the other books here. I had fun finding people who wanted to sponsor me, but reading is a pain. I'd rather spend my time playing — or solving the mystery about the fires."

As much as Nicky wanted to help with detective work, I knew he was supposed to be spending his library time on the Readathon. I decided to ignore his comment. "I'm sure we can find a *few* good books here," I said gently. I gestured at the shelves. "There must be something you like to read about."

"I like monsters," said Nicky, looking down at his shoes. "But I bet they don't have any good monster books *here*."

"Oh, yeah? How much do you want to bet? A hundred dollars? A thousand? A gazillion?"

Nicky grinned. "How about just a nickel?" he asked, pushing his hand into the pocket of his jeans. "That's all I have."

"No, I'm not going to bet you anything," I

said. "It wouldn't be fair, because I happen to *know* that this library has at least five great monster books."

"Really?" Nicky threw me a skeptical look.

"Really. Come on, I'll show you." I led him to the card catalog and showed him how to look up "Monsters." We wrote down the numbers of three of the books, and we were just checking the fourth when — the fire alarm went off.

"Not again!" I said.

"I didn't do it!" said Nicky quickly. "I was right here with you, the whole time."

"I know. Now let's get going. Can you head over to the door and line up with the other kids?" I gave him a nudge. "I'll be right there." I wanted to check all the nooks and crannies of the children's room to make sure no kids were left behind when we went outside. I saw Kristy taking Rosie to the line by the door, and we exchanged worried glances. Once again, I could smell smoke in the air. This was getting ridiculous, not to mention scary.

I had just checked the Raggedy Ann corner when I glanced up to see a frazzled-looking Miss Ellway dashing through the room. "Oh, my lord!" I whispered to myself. Where was Miss Ellway going? Was Claudia right in suspecting her? Had Miss Ellway set the fire —

and was she now running away from the scene of the crime?

I barely had time to think about the possibility before I saw Miss Ellway returning, this time carrying a fire extinguisher. "Don't worry, Mary Anne!" she cried, as she dashed past me. "It's just a small fire. I think we can put it out." Oops. Boy, did I feel bad.

I went back to checking the library for stray kids, just in case. Even if the fire was small, it would be safer to evacuate everyone. But by the time Kristy and I had lined up the kids, Ms. Feld told us that the fire was out and that everybody could return to whatever they had been doing.

I heaved a sigh of relief. The kids — and the books — were safe. But who had set the fire? Where had it been set, and what had been burned this time? I ran up the back stairs and into Mrs. Kishi's office, pretending to be upset. "Is the fire really out?" I asked. "Where was it? This is getting so scary!"

"Calm down, Mary Anne," said Mrs. Kishi. "Everything is all right. If you like, I'll show you where the fire was, so you can see for yourself." She led me back downstairs, to a trash can that sat outside one of the doors to the children's room, in the hall where the bathrooms are. The hallway had been temporarily blocked off with a row of chairs. "See?" she said. "No fire. The police asked me to block it off until they arrive. The fire department will come, too. Then, once the janitor cleans up this mess, nobody would ever guess there even *was* a fire."

And all the clues would be gone, too, I thought to myself. I leaned down to examine the contents of the trash can. All I saw at first were a few partially burned pieces of paper. Then I spotted something that made my heart race. A book! I looked closer, and saw the charred remains of a library copy of *Tom Sawyer*. I took a deep breath, stood up, and smiled at Mrs. Kishi. "I'm sorry I got so upset," I said. "These fires really frighten me."

"Me, too," she agreed. But the police don't seem to take them very seriously. They think they're just a series of pranks, and they say that the best thing to do is try to prevent future fires and just ignore these. The prankster probably wants attention, and it's best not to give it to him — or her."

I nodded. "Well, I better get back to work," I said. "Thanks for showing this to me. I feel much better."

I returned to the children's room and found Nicky. "Ready to find those books?" I asked. And for the next hour, I was busy with my job.

During that hour, though, something was nagging at me, as though I had forgotten something, or something was missing. I couldn't put my finger on what it was.

"Ready to go?" Kristy asked me at about five o'clock. "I'm going to walk Rosie home and then head for the meeting. Why don't you come with us?"

"Okay," I said, looking around. "I guess I'm done here." I *still* had the feeling I had forgotten something, but I tried to shake it off. I grabbed my jacket and put it on. I reached into my pocket for my gloves, and pulled out the book list the demonstrators had given me. Something made me unfold it and look it over, and then I realized what had been nagging at me. As I read the list, I swear I felt a light bulb turn on in my brain.

"Kristy!" I hissed, pulling her aside. "I have to show you something. It's about the fires!"

"Wait," she whispered. "Not in front of Rosie. Wait till we drop her off at home."

We left the library and walked quickly, hurrying Rosie along. As soon as we had seen her safely inside, Kristy turned to me. "What is it?" she asked.

"This," I said, shoving the list into her hands. "A list of books those demonstrators want to ban."

"So?" she said.

"Kristy, every one of the books that was burned is *on that list*."

Kristy looked shocked. Then she glanced at the list and nodded. "You're absolutely right. There's *Deenie*, and *A Light in the Attic*."

"And there's *Tom Sawyer*," I said. "That's the book that was burned today."

"I guess we have some new suspects," Kristy said grimly. "I thought those people were just book banners, and that was bad enough. But they might be book *burners*, too."

CHAPTER 10

"Mal will be so happy to hear that Nicky is off the suspect list," said Jessi. "Not that anyone ever really suspected him, but — well, you know."

Once again, Kristy had relaxed club rules. Even though it was an official BSC meeting, she was allowing us to start out by discussing something other than club business. Not only was she allowing it — she was pretty much *leading* the discussion. She and I had filled in the others on what had happened at the library that afternoon, and everybody was appalled. A third fire.

"I just can't believe this," said Shannon, who was reading through the book banner's list I had passed around. "I can't even figure out what could possibly be dangerous about some of these books."

"It all depends on how you look at things, I guess," said Stacey. "Some people seem to think the Bobbsey Twins are the only safe books to read."

"But, really," said Shannon. "This is ridiculous! I mean, *A Wrinkle in Time* is on this list. That's a great book."

"I know," said Stacey. "And what about *How to Eat Fried Worms*? I mean, that's just a harmless, funny book."

"*We* think so," I said. "But apparently some people disagree."

"Yeah," said Kristy. "And one of them believes that it's better to *burn* those books than to let kids read them."

"We don't know that for *sure*," I said. "I mean, I guess the book banners are our major suspects. Nicky's off the hook, and now I'm almost positive that Miss Ellway is innocent, too." I had told everybody about seeing her run toward the fire with the extinguisher. "But would they really endanger the whole library — and all the people in it — just to make a point?"

"They seem to feel pretty strongly about their cause," said Kristy.

"That doesn't mean that they're criminals," argued Stacey. "But maybe we should do a little investigating. Maybe we can talk to them and find out more about what they're trying to do."

"Oh, sure," said Claudia. "Like we're going

to walk up to them and say, 'Excuse me, but did you guys happen to set those fires in the library?' "

Stacey made a face at Claud. "That's not what I meant, silly. Maybe we could pretend to be from our school paper or something."

"That's perfect!" I exclaimed. "They *want* publicity. That's the whole point of demonstrating. Plus, they've written letters to the *Stoneybrook News*. They would probably love the idea of more exposure."

The phone started ringing then, and we were busy for the next few minutes answering calls and setting up jobs. But before the meeting ended, we had decided on a plan.

First, Claudia and Stacey would approach the demonstrators and just talk to them a little, asking casual questions about why they wanted to ban books and finding out who the members of the group were. Then Jessi and Shannon would do some spying: following the members as they left the library and trying to find out what other types of activities they were involved in. Finally, Kristy and I would pose as reporters for the SMS newspaper, and try to ask a few more probing questions.

"The more we know about them, the better," said Kristy. "And if we're *really* lucky, maybe we'll come up with some real evidence — evidence we could take to the police."

I was full of energy when I left the meeting that afternoon. It felt good to have a plan — a plan for *doing* something that might lead to ending the fires in the library.

Kristy and I had agreed to wait for a few days before we approached the demonstrators in our "school newspaper-reporter" roles. We needed to hear what the others found out first.

At our Friday meeting, Claudia and Stacey told us that talking to the demonstrators had been pretty frustrating. "They didn't want to discuss anything except how terrible those books on the list are, and how they poison children's minds," said Stacey. "I asked that woman in the green hat why *A Light in the Attic* was on the list, and she started to lecture me about profanity and violence. I tried to argue with her, since I didn't really remember any of that kind of stuff in the book, but she just kept talking louder and louder."

"I didn't find out too much, either," said Claudia. She was poking through a bag of M&M's as she spoke, picking out all the brown ones. She insists that the brown ones taste best. "I hung back and watched everybody. I tried to figure out what kind of people they were, and if they were related. Like, if any of them were married couples or whatever. Anyway," she went on, popping a whole handful of brown M&M's into her mouth, "the main thing I discovered was — "

Just then, the phone rang, and Kristy held up a hand to Claudia. "Hold that thought," she said. She picked up the phone and said, "Baby-sitters Club. Can I help you?"

The call was from Mrs. Hill, who was looking for a Saturday night sitter for Norman and Sarah. I checked the record book and saw that Shannon and Stacey were the only ones free. "You take it, Stacey," said Shannon. "I was thinking about going to the movies that night anyway."

Kristy called Mrs. Hill back and told her that Stacey would be there at six on Saturday. Then she hung up and turned to Claudia. "Okay," she said. "So, what were you saying? It sounded like you found out something important."

"Well, it's important to *me*," said Claudia, giggling. "And maybe to Stacey. But I doubt the rest of you will think it's very meaningful." She picked out a red M&M (her next favorite color) and ate it. "What I observed was that the book banners have very little fashion sense." She grinned.

"*Claudia!*" said Kristy, cracking up. "I don't believe you."

Stacey picked up a pillow and bopped Claudia on the head. "You're a nut," she said, giggling.

"I'm serious!" protested Claudia. "You should have *seen* some of the outfits these people were wearing. I mean, I wouldn't even call them *outfits*. Nothing matched, everything clashed, and they obviously don't know a *thing* about coordinating accessories."

We cracked up. "Oh, I can just see it," said Jessi, wiping tears of laughter from her eyes. "We'll go to the police and say, 'Book these people. They're in serious violation of every fashion rule, including hem length and color composition.' They'd *have* to take us seriously."

Claudia pretended to be offended. "Well, you all may not think it means much, but personally, *I* happen to think it's a crime to dress like that."

Once we got over our giggles, Jessi and Shannon made their report. "Well," began Jessi, "I can't say we learned too much either. We followed the woman in the green hat for awhile, but she just did normal stuff like grocery shopping and picking up dry cleaning. She seems to live over by the elementary school, in a regular-looking house."

"We did notice one suspicious thing," said Shannon. "Or at least *I* thought it was suspicious. After she picked up her dry cleaning, she stopped to look in the window of the bookstore, and after she had looked for awhile she whipped out a notebook and wrote something down."

"Oh, no," said Kristy. "I wonder if they're going to try to burn down the bookstore next."

"I don't know if they're going to burn down anything," said Jessi. "I didn't get the feeling that they're *criminals*. They all seem like regular moms and dads. We followed one of the men for a while, and all he did was pick up his little girl at the day-care center. I know it's important to keep an eye on these people, but I don't think we should forget about looking for *other* suspects, too."

Kristy and I decided to check the library on Saturday, to see if the demonstrators were there. If they were, we would try to interview them. If not, we would wait until Monday.

"We're in luck!" said Kristy, as we neared the library at about ten o'clock on Saturday morning. Sure enough, a small group of demonstrators was clustered near the library entrance.

I saw some new faces, men and women I hadn't noticed on other days, and figured they must be people who only had time to demonstrate on weekends. But I saw some familiar faces, too. The man with the sign was there, and so was the woman with the green hat. Kristy and I held a quick discussion and decided to approach her first.

"Excuse me," said Kristy. "I'm Kristy Thomas and this is Mary Anne Spier. We're writing a story on book-banning for our school newspaper, and we were wondering if we could interview you."

"Me?" asked the woman. "Well, it would be my pleasure. My name is Bertha Dow. That's D-O-W. Mrs. Bertha Dow." She handed us copies of the list, along with a couple of pamphlets that looked as if they had been run off on a mimeograph machine.

Kristy nodded at me, and I gulped. It was time to ask some questions. I pulled a pad and pencil out of my backpack, and began. "What do you hope to accomplish by demonstrating?" I asked.

That was all Mrs. Dow needed to get started. She talked for fifteen minutes solid. I pretended to scribble notes, and I nodded and said "Mm hmm," but most of what she said sounded pretty familiar. It was the same stuff she had told Stacey.

I could see that Kristy was growing impatient. Suddenly, she burst in with a question, a question I never would have asked. "Have you ever burned any books?" she asked.

The woman looked a little surprised. I, for one, was shocked. But I was even more astonished when the woman answered.

"Yes, I have," she said. "I was part of a public demonstration in North Carolina, many years ago. We set fire to a pile of offensive books, thinking it was the best way to draw attention to our cause. Some of us were arrested, though, and the publicity was awful. I realized then that burning books is not a good idea, and I've never done it again." She smiled sweetly at Kristy, who could only stare. "I think there are better ways to get our point across."

Kristy was just standing there with her mouth open. I put my pencil and notebook away, thanked Mrs. Dow for her time, and pulled Kristy down the street.

"I can't believe she actually admitted she burned books!" said Kristy. "I mean, even if they aren't the ones setting the fires. What an awful thing to do!"

I agreed. "It *is* awful. But I believed her when she said she would never do it again. I'm not crazy about those people, but somehow I don't think they're setting the fires."

"So we're at a dead end again, aren't we?" asked Kristy.

"I guess," I said. "But I'm not ready to give up." I wanted to solve the case more than ever — before another fire was set.

CHAPTER 11

Sunday

Well, we didn't get a whole lot accomplished today, but we had fun. I saw parts of Stoneybrook I never knew about, and we met some neat people. I can't say we're any closer to knowing who is setting the fires, though....

Shannon picked up Rosie Wilder at home that afternoon. Kristy couldn't sit for Rosie, so Shannon was taking her place. It was a chilly afternoon, but the sun was out, and Shannon was in a good mood. "I hear you're doing great in the Readathon," Shannon said, as she and Rosie walked toward the library. "Do you think you have a chance of winning the prize for your grade?"

"Definitely," said Rosie. "I'm good at winning contests, like spelling bees and things. Did you ever see all the ribbons and plaques I have at home?"

Shannon shook her head.

"I'll show them to you later," said Rosie, skipping along. "After we go to the library and get some more books, that is. I finished all these already." She showed Shannon a pile of five or six books.

"Very impressive," said Shannon. She wasn't put off by Rosie's boasting. Winning prizes was just a part of life for Rosie.

When they reached the library, they found Claudia there with Nicky. I was there, too, working. The children's room wasn't quite as busy as usual, since it was a Sunday, but it was still full of activity. Ms. Feld was trying to listen to reports, make up a bulletin-board display, and write up overdue notices. Miss Ellway was checking out books and helping new kids sign up for library cards.

"Is the children's room always open on Sundays?" asked Shannon, sitting down at a table in the nonfiction room with Claudia and me. Rosie and Nicky wandered off to look at books.

"Just for a few hours," I said, "but with the Readathon going on the kids really make use of the time. I can't believe how many of them are here."

Shannon snuck a few glances at Miss Ellway. "She doesn't *look* like a firebug," she whispered to me.

"I know," I said. "But you know what I just thought of? I was talking to her before, and she mentioned that her brother owns a hardware store in town. That means there's at least one other Ellway around. Maybe somebody *else* in the Ellway family is starting the fires."

Claudia raised her eyebrows. "Good point, Mary Anne. They would all have a stake in destroying this place, wouldn't they?"

"Shh!" I said. "I don't want Miss Ellway to hear us."

"But if they want the land back," said Shannon, "they're not doing a very good job of burning down the library."

"That's true," said Claudia. "Maybe those little fires are supposed to throw people off the track. You know, everybody gets used to them, and then — boom! — the *big* fire is set."

"Hmmm," said Shannon. "You could be right."

Nicky's head popped up behind Claudia, startling us all. "If she's right," he said, "we better find out who those other Ellways are!"

"Nicky!" said Claudia. "Were you eavesdropping?"

Nicky blushed. "I — I was just walking by," he said.

"So was I," piped up Rosie, from behind me. "And I agree with Nicky. What are we doing sitting around here, when there are leads we could be following?"

Shannon, Claudia, and I exchanged amused glances. "What about your reading?" Shannon asked Rosie. "I thought you wanted to win that prize."

Rosie shrugged. "I'd rather solve this mystery," she said. "So, what do we do first?"

"Well, we can't just walk up to Miss Ellway and ask her for all her relatives' names and addresses," I said, thinking out loud.

"What if we could find an obituary for old Mr. Ellway?" asked Shannon. "They usually list the relatives in those."

"You're right!" said Claudia. "And I bet we can find the obituary with the microfiche, upstairs. My mom showed me how to use it. It has all the newspapers on it, going way back."

And that was the last I saw of Claudia, Shannon, Nicky, and Rosie that day. They headed upstairs, but I had to stay in the children's room and work. It wasn't until later that evening, when Shannon called me, that I found out what they had done for the rest of the afternoon.

The obituary was easy to find. It was in the *Stoneybrook News* of November 13, 1943, along with a longer article about Mr. Ellway's life. Theodore Ellway, the four of them discovered, had been a big shot in Stoneybrook. He had made a fortune building houses, and he had died a very rich man. He had given a lot of money and land to the town, but many of his gifts had strings attached. For example, he had donated a little park, which would only belong to the town for as long as the people in the town agreed to feed the ducks that visited a pond in the park. "That's dumb," said Nicky, when he read that part of the obituary.

"I think it's neat," said Rosie. "It just means he cared about the ducks and didn't want them to starve."

"What about his children and grandchildren, though?" asked Claudia. "He didn't seem to care if *they* starved."

"It's true that he didn't leave them much," said Shannon. "He seems to have thought it was important for them to be independent. See, here's a quote from him." She pointed to a paragraph in the article.

" 'I worked hard for every penny I earned,' said Ellway,' " Claudia read out loud. "Then here, he said, 'I believe that hard work builds character.' I think he was worried about what would happen to his descendants if money was just handed to them."

"So, who *are* his descendants?" asked Nicky.

"Well," said Claudia. "I only see one name: His son, Theodore Ellway the second. Then it mentions a granddaughter and a grandson. There is also a great-granddaughter and a great-grandson, infant children of Theodore Ellway the third."

Nicky scribbled away. "Boy, they like that name Theodore," he said. "How do you spell that, anyway?"

"Forget about Theodore the second," called Shannon, who had been working at another microfiche machine. "I guess he was Miss Ellway's father, and he died in 1974. But it gives his kids' names in his obituary, *and* his grandkids' names. His kids are Miriam — that's our Miss Ellway — and Theodore Ellway the third. And I guess Theodore the third has two kids named Rosa and — surprise! — Theodore the fourth."

"Wow," said Claudia. "This is pretty confusing." She thought for a moment. "I guess Theodore the third would be middle-aged by now, right?"

"At *least* middle-aged," said Shannon. "He's Miss Ellway's brother, and she's no spring chicken."

"Isn't her brother the one who owns the hardware store?" asked Rosie. "I bet that's the one my dad goes to. I go with him sometimes. It's called Ted's Tools. Ted is short for Theodore, right? There's a nice man there, and a nice lady, too. I bet that's his wife."

"Okay!" said Claudia. "So, we know where our first stop will be. But how do we find the other Ellways — his son and daughter?"

"Can't we just check the phone book for their addresses?" asked Shannon.

Claudia snapped her fingers. "Right!" she said. "Okay, we're all set. Ready, everybody?"

They left the library and headed downtown to the hardware store. It's open on Sunday for homeowners who are working on weekend do-it-yourself projects, and lots of people were there. Claudia pretended to be interested in some light fixtures, and she held a long conversation with Ted Ellway. (She knew he was Ted Ellway, because he was wearing a nametag.) Meanwhile, Shannon, Rosie, and Nicky browsed around the store. It's a neat place, an old-fashioned hardware store with a million different things on the shelves: nuts and bolts and nails and glue and fishing line and every kind of tool you can imagine. The aisles are narrow, so customers have to squeeze by each other as they hunt for spare parts for their lawnmowers or new reflectors for their bicycles.

Shannon told me later that Mrs. Ellway (her name tag said "Dottie") was a good-natured woman who appeared to be at home behind the cash register. She joked with every customer, and seemed to know them all by name. Claudia found that Ted Ellway was really nice, too. Instead of treating her like a kid, he took her seriously and spent a long time helping her find the right kind of light fixture. She said later that she felt rotten when she told him he really didn't have what she wanted. "I couldn't help it, though," she said. "I didn't have any money with me, and besides, I didn't really *need* the thing anyway."

The four of them left Ted's Tools, Rosie and Nicky clutching lollipops that Dottie had handed them. "Didn't I tell you? They're really nice in there," said Rosie, eyeing her purple lollipop.

"I'm going back tomorrow," said Nicky, taking a lick at his green one.

Claudia looked at Shannon and shrugged.

"They sure don't seem like people who would burn down a library," she said. "But maybe their son and daughter will turn out to be terrible people. Let's check the phone book and find out where they live."

It only took a few minutes at a nearby phone booth to find the addresses for Ted the Fourth and Rosa Ellway. Ted the Fourth lived in a ritzy area of town, not Kristy and Shannon's neighborhood but an even fancier one. And Rosa lived near the vet's office.

They headed to Rosa's place, first, since it was nearer. It turned out that she ran Ellway's Kennel, where people could leave their dogs and cats while they were on vacation. When Shannon and the others arrived, they found a cheerful red-haired woman in the yard, playing fetch with a black-and-white puppy. Shannon pretended to be looking for a place to board her dog, Astrid. After just one short conversation about dogs and puppies she realized Rosa was just as nice as her parents.

As for Ted the Fourth, he turned out to be a great guy, too. Not that they met him. They found that out from the gardener, who was trimming the long, long hedge that ran along the long, long driveway to Ted's huge mansion.

"Mr. Ellway? He's the greatest boss a man could have," said the gardener. "His wife is terrific, too. She's the one with all the money, but she's just a regular gal. Usually she's right out here with me, hauling brush."

Claudia threw up her hands as they walked away from the Ellway mansion. "We did all that work," she said, with a laugh, "and all we ended up with is the news that the Ellways are wonderful people!"

"And we were hoping for arsonists and murderers and thieves," said Shannon, giggling. "What a shame."

Nicky and Rosie started giggling, too, though Shannon wasn't sure they understood the joke. Their investigation hadn't led them anywhere, but at least, as Shannon said later, they'd had fun trying.

CHAPTER 12

I laughed when Shannon told me about her adventures with Rosie, Nicky, and Claudia, but I felt glum after we hung up.

Our investigation was going nowhere. Oh, sure, we had a few leads, but none of them was panning out. The mystery was confusing and scary, and it worried me.

I had been having bad dreams lately. Dreams about fires burning out of control. In one of the dreams, the burning library was a big house where all my favorite children's-book characters lived. Mrs. Piggle-Wiggle had to jump out of a high window, while the Runaway Bunny squirmed out of a low one and Ramona Quimby stood on the lawn, wearing her pajamas and crying. It was horrible.

I was losing sleep because of the dreams, which meant that I was feeling foggy during school. I was still finishing my homework and passing quizzes, but during class time I often felt as if my head were wrapped in cotton gauze.

I was feeling that way on Monday during math class. We were supposed to be working on a problem about a man who was selling apples at $3.25 a pound and another man who wanted to buy two and a quarter pounds of them, and none of it was making any sense to me. I sat chewing on my eraser, hoping the teacher would call on somebody else.

And then the fire alarm went off. "Fire drill!" yelled Alan Gray, this obnoxious boy who happens to be in my math class. "Don't panic, boys and girls. Just line up and walk this way." He stood up and started doing this silly walk toward the front of the class.

My teacher, Ms. Frost, glared at him. "Please sit down, Alan," she said. "Fire drills are not a joking matter. Class, you know the procedure. Please line up and get ready to leave the classroom — *quietly.*"

I gave a huge sigh and closed my notebook. A fire drill was the last thing I needed that day. For one thing, it was just plain boring. We would all line up and file out of the school, stand outside in the freezing cold for a few minutes, and then file back in. Some kids would clown around, and the rest of us would try to ignore them.

For another thing, I was beginning to feel

that my life had been one big fire alarm lately.

I lined up with the others and followed Ms. Frost out the door and down the hall. The hall was packed with kids shuffling along, jostling each other and giggling.

"Can I stop at my locker, Ms. Frost?" asked a girl named Tiffany.

"I'm afraid not," said Ms. Frost. "We're supposed to head straight for the main parking lot."

"What if somebody needs to — you know, use the facilities?" asked Alan Gray, with a wicked grin.

"Alan, are you trying to tell me that you need to go to the bathroom?" asked Ms. Frost, loudly enough so all the kids in the area could hear her. There was a lot of snickering, and Alan actually blushed.

"Um, no," he mumbled. "It was just a hypothetical question."

"Well, from now on, I'll ask you to hold the hypothetical questions until we're safely out of the building," said Ms. Frost. She sounded firm, but she was smiling a little.

I spotted Kristy emerging from her social studies classroom, and I called to her and waved. "Meet you by the fence!" she called back, and I knew exactly where she meant. My friends and I have a spot where we meet sometimes, before or after school. I knew I'd probably find the other members of the BSC there once we were safely outside.

My class made its way through the crowded hallway. At one point, Alan Gray and some other boys started to make mooing noises, as if we were a herd of cows. "Git along, little dogie," said Alan, smacking another boy on the rear. That led to a short shoving match, and someone trampled on my toes, which made me squeal.

"*Mr.* Gray!" said Ms. Frost. "This is your last warning. Do I need to report you to Mr. Kingbridge?"

Mr. Kingbridge is the assistant principal, and being sent to him is worse than being sent to the principal, whose name is Mr. Taylor. Mr. Kingbridge is in charge of discipline, and he has the power to suspend kids who get into trouble.

Alan and the other boys stopped mooing, and the hall was quieter until we reached the doors. Then the boys started shoving again, and fooling around. Alan held the door open for another boy. "After you," he said politely. When the boy tried to walk through the door, Alan stopped holding it and tried to squeeze through at the same time.

"Boys, boys," said Mr. Fiske, one of the English teachers. "I know this seems like an opportunity to make fools of yourselves, but that's actually not the point of the exercise. What we're trying to do here is get everyone out of the building as quickly and as quietly as we can."

Alan was blushing again. Mr. Fiske held the door for him, and he stepped out without a word. The rest of us followed. It was wonderful to be out of that hot, crowded hall. I knew I was going to start freezing soon, without my coat, but for a second the cold air felt great. The parking lot was full of kids who seemed to be milling about aimlessly. We're supposed to stay with our classes during a fire drill, but nobody ever does. I headed for the fence, and found Kristy, Claudia, and Stacey waiting there already. "Hey, Mary Anne," said Kristy. "We have almost enough people for a BSC meeting!"

"Here come Jessi and Mal," said Stacey. "They look upset."

"Isn't this awful?" said Jessi, as she and Mal neared us.

"What, having a fire drill in the middle of social studies?" asked Kristy. "I can think of worse things."

"Kristy, it's not just a fire drill," said Mal.

"What do you mean?"

At that moment, I heard the sound of sirens, and my stomach did a flip-flop.

"It's a real fire," said Mal, as three fire engines pulled into the parking lot.

"Oh, my lord!" exclaimed Claudia. She began to search in her pocketbook, found a kind of mushy-looking bar and offered it around, but nobody wanted any. We were too busy staring at the fire fighters. Several of them leapt off the trucks and started uncoiling hoses. Others grabbed axes from the toolboxes on the trucks and dashed into the school.

"This is for real," I said to nobody in particular. "It's not a fire drill, and I'm pretty sure it's not a dream." I stopped to pinch myself on the arms. Maybe it *was* just a dream. But no, the pinch hurt enough to make my eyes water. What was going *on*? Why were there fires in every building I spent time in lately?

"I smell smoke," said Kristy, sniffing the air.

"I do, too," said Claudia, taking a bite of her chocolate bar. "Are you guys sure you don't want any of this? I think I have some Twizzlers, too." She started to root around in her bag again.

Another fire truck pulled up, and more fire fighters jumped out and ran into the building. "Whoa, this is *serious*," said Stacey.

Just then, Mr. Taylor climbed up onto one of the fire trucks, holding the fire chief's bullhorn. "Attention," he said. "May I have your attention?"

The noise level in the parking lot, which had

been very high, dropped off. I noticed that even Alan Gray and his friends turned to listen to Mr. Taylor.

"There is a fire in the school," began Mr. Taylor.

"Duh," said Kristy, under her breath. I turned to her and frowned. Then I turned back to Mr. Taylor.

"On the advice of the fire department, I am canceling classes for the rest of the day."

A huge cheer went up, led by Alan Gray. Mr. Taylor gestured for silence. "Our emergency evacuation plan specifies that you will be escorted to the high school, to wait in the gym until your parents can be alerted to the circumstances. A bulletin will go out over the radio, local businesses will be called, and the phones in the high school will be available for use."

"This is exciting," Mal whispered.

I knew what she meant. It *was* kind of exciting. But it was upsetting, too. I can't deny that being let out of school early was fun, but not if it meant that the school was going to burn down. I may not love everything about SMS, but I wouldn't want the place to be destroyed.

"Girls and boys," finished Mr. Taylor, "I hope I can trust you to behave like mature young adults. Please follow your teachers' instructions, and make your way to the high school in an orderly fashion."

"What about our coats?" asked Kristy.

"And our notebooks and stuff?" asked Mal.

"I guess we have to leave them here," said Claudia. "Come on, let's go. After we talk to our parents, maybe we can go to my house and make some popcorn."

We followed the crowd to the high school. When we arrived, the gym was already a mob scene. There were long lines at the phones by the school office, too. But eventually my friends and I got in touch with our parents and told them we would be at Claud's — except for Mal, who was told to come home.

By the time we left the high school, we had heard lots of rumors and a few facts about the fire. The rumors, which were probably started by Alan Gray and his friends, were wild: that the school had blown up right after we had left, and that we would all receive passing grades for middle school without attending any further classes.

The facts, which we heard from Ms. Frost, were that the fire had started in a classroom near the school library. The library had suffered smoke and water damage, and the classroom would be out of use for at least a month.

Later, at Claudia's, we munched popcorn and discussed the afternoon's events. We wondered if the fire was related to the fires at the library, and whether the book banners could be responsible after all. The school fire certainly didn't seem to have anything to do with the Ellways, and there was no way Nicky Pike could have started it, which let him off the hook once and for all. Not that any of us still thought he might be guilty.

After awhile, we stopped talking about the mystery and concentrated on our popcorn and some magazines Claudia passed around. I guess we needed a break from thinking about the mystery. But the break didn't last long. At five-fifteen, Shannon showed up for our BSC meeting, and Kristy announced that that day's meeting would be focused on the mystery of the fires. "No more fooling around," she said. "It's time to solve this case."

CHAPTER 13

"I hereby call this meeting to order," said Kristy solemnly. She was sitting up straight in the director's chair, and she looked very serious and very official. "And I hereby declare this meeting an *emergency* meeting."

Claudia, who was rummaging around underneath her bed, looked up. "Does that mean we can't eat the chocolate-covered pretzels I got for today?" she asked. "They're right here." She pulled out a long, flat box marked "Kaligrufy pens." "I have some jelly beans, too. And some plain pretzels for you, Stace." She smiled at Stacey.

"Go ahead and pass them around, Claud," said Kristy. "We need to keep our energy up, right?" She grinned at Claudia, and helped herself to a chocolate-covered pretzel. "These look great," she said. "Anyway," she went on, sitting up straight again, "as I said, it's time to crack down on this mystery. The library could burn down any day, fires are starting in *other* places, too, and — well, I hate to say this, but Mary Anne is losing it."

I ducked my head and blushed. Kristy and I had had a long talk on the phone the night before, and I had told her about my bad dreams. I cried a little during the conversation, too. I knew she was worried about me, and that was nice. But she was embarrassing me by discussing my mental state in front of everyone else.

"If we don't solve this case soon, Mary Anne is going to have a nervous breakdown," said Kristy, "and where would that leave the BSC?"

"*Kristy,*" I said, blushing even harder. "Don't listen to her, you guys," I said to the rest of my friends. "I'm fine — really!"

"Well, I'm not," said Jessi, from her seat on the floor. She was stretching, as usual, and her arms looked graceful as she bent from side to side. "I missed a step in ballet class the other day and almost took a really bad fall. I can't seem to concentrate at all lately."

"Me, neither," said Stacey, who was sitting on the bed between Claud and me. "I got five questions wrong on my math quiz on Friday. Mr. Zizmore asked me if I was sick."

"You know," said Claudia thoughtfully, "I've been kind of in a fog, too. I tried to make papier-mâché on Saturday, and I couldn't remember the recipe for it."

"I know I've had a few bad dreams myself," said Shannon.

"Well," said Kristy, "obviously Mary Anne isn't the only one who's upset about the fires. The question is, what are we going to do about it?" She frowned a little and tugged at her visor.

Jessi raised her hand, as if she were in school. "Go over all our clues?" she asked tentatively.

"Good idea," said Kristy, nodding.

"Think about each fire — where it was burning and *what* was burning," suggested Shannon.

"And write down the suspects' names and make notes about whether they're still suspects or not," added Claudia. "Nancy Drew does that sometimes. You can use that pad of paper on my desk."

"Great," said Kristy. "Okay, let's start with a list of suspects. First, there's Miss Ellway."

"I'm almost *positive* it isn't her," I said quickly.

"I know," said Kristy. "But we're just putting everybody on this list. Later we can cross them off."

"Well, in that case," said Jessi, "we'd have to include Nicky Pike, too."

Kristy nodded and made a note on the pad.

"And the book banners, of course," I said. I was trying to concentrate on what we were doing, but my mind seemed to be running off in directions of its own. The idea of making a list had jogged something in my brain.

"Is that everybody?" asked Kristy.

"Everybody *I* can think of," said Stacey. "But I'm sure there's somebody we haven't thought of, since none of the people on that list seem to be real suspects. We could probably cross every one of them off, based on what we've found out so far."

Kristy looked deflated. "Well, let's move on to the next thing," she said. "We'll list the fires and make notes about them. First, there was the fire in the bathroom and *Deenie* was burned." She made some notes. "That fire wasn't too bad. It was put out right away."

"We never *did* find out which bathroom it was in," said Jessi. "Wasn't Logan supposed to check the boy's room?"

Kristy made a note. "Good point," she said. "We can look into that."

"The next fire was in the trash can outside the back door of the children's room," said Claudia. "Someone used lighter fluid to start that fire." She shivered. "That one was a little more serious," she added.

"Was that when *A Light in the Attic* was burned?" asked Jessi.

"Yup," said Stacey. "I remember because I talked to the book banner lady afterward."

"And the third fire," said Shannon. "Wasn't that in another trash can, in the hall by the bathrooms? And *Tom Sawyer* was the book, right?"

As the others talked, I had been thinking *hard*. I was picturing the children's room, remembering how it was laid out and how the books were shelved. I also kept thinking about that word "list," and why it seemed to mean something. Suddenly, I gave a huge gasp.

"What?" asked Kristy. "Mary Anne, are you okay? What is it?"

"I just figured something out," I said. "Something really, really big."

"What?" asked Kristy.

"Okay," I said. "This is going to sound nuts, but here goes. I think the fires are being set in a pattern. Each book was burned near the place where it was shelved. At least, the Shel Silverstein book was, and so was *Tom Sawyer*. We definitely have to find out which bathroom the Judy Blume book was burned in."

"I can ask right now," said Claudia. She reached for the phone, called her mom, and reported to us, "It was in the boy's bathroom."

"It fits!" I said. "And that also tells us that the firebug is probably male, since he was able to go in and out of the boy's bathroom without being noticed."

"Mary Anne," said Kristy, trying to sound patient, "I know this is leading up to something, but I'm not sure I get it yet."

"That's because there's another part to it," I said. "I've been sitting here thinking about lists, and suddenly I realized something. All three of those books are on the fifth-grade reading list!"

"Wow," breathed Jessi. "This is wild."

"I just thought of another pattern!" said Stacey suddenly. "All the fires were set on Wednesdays. I'm sure of it, because we always had BSC meetings right after the fires."

"The fire at school wasn't on a Wednesday," said Claudia.

"No, but I don't think that fire is related," I said. "Let's put that one aside for now. What we have to do is crack the code, and figure out where the next fire will be."

"This is awesome!" said Claudia. "Now I *really* feel like Nancy Drew."

"Are there any other trash cans in the children's room?" asked Jessi.

"I can't remember," I said.

"I mean, if there's one near another book on the fifth-grade list, all we have to do is watch that spot on Wednesday," Jessi went on. She jumped to her feet. "Let's go check out the library right now!"

"We can't," I said. "It's almost six, and the children's room is about to close. We'll have to go tomorrow."

I couldn't believe the way the pieces to our theory had fallen together. We finished up our meeting (we *had* managed to take care of a few baby-sitting calls, too), promising to meet at the fence as soon as we got out of school the next day.

It didn't take us long to figure out that there was only one spot left in the children's room for the firebug to try. It was another trash can, tucked away near the reference books in the nonfiction room. "This has to be the place!" I said. I flipped quickly through the fifth-grade reading list and pointed to a book about Abraham Lincoln, with a star next to it, signifying that it was highly recommended. "And I bet that's the book," I said. I led my friends to the spot where the book was shelved, and showed it to them.

We grinned at each other and Kristy gave me a high-five. "I have a feeling we're on to something," she said. "As long as our firebug sticks to his pattern, we'll be able to squash him ourselves."

CHAPTER 14

The moment the last bell rang at school the next day, I ran to my locker, grabbed my jacket and headed out to meet my friends at our spot near the fence. Logan was already there, waiting for me. I had called him the night before to tell him about our plan to stake out the library, and he was excited about it. Better yet, he was going to be able to join us, since the team didn't have a game that afternoon.

"Hey," he said, in his warm Southern drawl. He smiled at me, and I felt a familiar flutter in my stomach. I'd been so busy lately I'd almost forgotten how much I missed Logan. I smiled back at him, and he leaned down to kiss me.

"Come on, you guys. There's no time for that stuff," said Kristy, from behind me. She grinned at us. "We're on a case, remember?"

Logan and I laughed. "Okay, boss," said

Logan. "We're ready when you are."

Stacey and Claud showed up then. They were giggling over something that had just happened in the hall, but Kristy didn't give them a chance to tell us about it. "Hey, you guys," she said. "We're going to be on a stake-out today. We're *supposed* to look unobtrusive. You know, like we blend in with our surroundings." She gave their outfits a critical look.

Claudia was wearing a big white shirt over a bright pink jumpsuit. Her earrings, also bright pink, were in the shape of flamingos. On her feet were pink high-tops. Stacey was wearing a red miniskirt, a red-and-white striped shirt, red heart-shaped earrings, and short black boots.

Stacey and Claud inspected each other's outfits. "I think you look awesome," said Claud.

"You look pretty good yourself," said Stacey, "but I already told you that at lunchtime."

They giggled. Kristy glared.

"They look okay, Kristy," I said. "Everybody's used to seeing them dressed like that. If they tried to blend in with their surroundings, *then* they'd look suspicious."

"I guess you're right," said Kristy. "Couldn't you at least take off those earrings, though?" she asked Claudia.

"What? And de-accessorize my whole outfit?"

Jessi and Mal arrived then. "I just came by to wish you guys good luck," said Mal. "I really, really wish I could come with you, but my parents would have a fit. I can't believe I still have to go straight home from school every day."

"We'll call you the second we have any news," I promised.

"Let's get going," said Kristy impatiently. "Shannon said she would meet us in the children's room, and she's probably already there. And anyway, the firebug isn't going to wait for us to arrive — know what I mean?"

That was all it took to get us going. We walked over to the library in a group, but I have to admit that Logan and I dawdled a little, walking a bit more slowly and staying behind everybody else. "I've missed you, Mary Anne," Logan murmured. We were holding hands, and it felt wonderful to be walking next to him.

"I've missed you, too," I said. For a moment I thought about how awful the past weeks might have been if I hadn't gotten involved in the Readathon. By now I probably would have worked my way through every sad movie in the video store, and I would be a soggy mess from crying for hours every afternoon.

The library was packed when we arrived. In addition to the regular Readathon kids, a preschool class was there: about thirteen little kids who were playing in the puppet theatre.

Charlotte Johanssen was there, with Jessi's sister Becca. They were sitting in the Raggedy Ann corner, reading. Norman Hill was working at a table with a stack of books in front of him. Nicky Pike and Sean Addison were avoiding the books, as usual, and playing with a wooden puzzle. Vanessa Pike was sitting near the poetry section, leafing through a book and making notes.

Miss Ellway was at the checkout desk, and Ms. Feld seemed to be everywhere at once. I watched as she helped one of the preschoolers tie a shoe, picked up a pile of books someone had left in the middle of the floor, and listened to a boy report on a book he had read, all in the space of about two minutes.

My friends and I headed for the reference area, after I had checked in with Ms. Feld. I was supposed to be working that afternoon, but I figured I could help with the stakeout, too. We were clustered near the encyclopedias when Stacey spoke up. "There are too many of us here," she said. "We'll probably scare the firebug off. Maybe we should split up."

"Good idea," I replied. "In fact, I was thinking we should keep an eye on the area near the bathrooms. What if the firebug fools us and returns to the scene of his first crime?"

"I'll go hang out near the boys' bathroom," offered Logan.

"I'll watch that other trash can by the door," said Claudia. "You never know. He might try that place, too."

Stacey decided to keep Claudia company, so that left Kristy, Shannon, Jessi, and me in the reference area. We spread out a little and pretended to be busy looking things up. Kristy grabbed a dictionary, and Jessi pulled out volume seven of the encyclopedia. I looked around to see if any kids needed me, and soon I was helping Corrie Addison choose a biography to read. Shannon hovered nearby, trying to act busy, too. We were all watching the trash can, but we made sure none of us was too close to it. We wanted the firebug to think he could do his dirty work without being seen.

Once I had finished with Corrie, nobody else seemed to need my help, so I took up a post for the stakeout. The kids went about their business, ignoring us completely. I saw Becca and Charlotte giggling together over a picture in one of their books. I heard a couple of kids I didn't know talking about which books were the shortest, and exchanging tips on how to answer the quiz that Ms. Feld gave

130

on each book. Vanessa Pike was in her own little world in the poetry corner. At one point I saw her looking dreamily out the window as if she were composing yet another poem of her own.

About half an hour after we had started the stakeout, I spotted Sean Addison as he entered the reference area. I was about to approach him to ask whether he needed any help, when Kristy put her hand on my arm and stopped me. We watched together as Sean went straight to the biography section and pulled out the book on Abraham Lincoln. I recognized its cover, and I let out a tiny gasp. Kristy glared at me and shook her head.

Sean looked around, as if he had heard my gasp, but we had ducked behind the card catalog. The next thing I saw made my heart race. I didn't want to believe my eyes, but there was no doubt about what Sean was doing.

He walked to the trash can, looked around furtively, and lowered the book into it. Then he reached into his jacket pocket and pulled out a small white can. He squirted its contents over the book, and then he stuck the can back into his pocket. From another pocket he pulled a pack of matches. He took one out of the pack and struck it.

It all happened so fast! I felt as if I were stuck in one of my nightmares. Sean was about to set a book on fire, but I couldn't seem to move my arms or legs. My voice wasn't working either, so I couldn't even call out to him.

Luckily, Kristy was on the ball. Just after Sean struck the match, and just *before* he dropped it into the trash can, Kristy leapt out of our hiding spot, grabbed Sean's arm, and blew out the match in his hand.

The firebug had been caught.

Sean looked stunned. "I was just — " he started to say, but Kristy interrupted him.

"We saw what you were doing," she said firmly. "We're going to have to take you to Mrs. Kishi's office, Sean." She began to lead him away from the trash can.

Sean looked as if he were about to cry.

"It's going to be all right," I said quickly. "We'll come with you, and you can tell us why you did it." Kristy and I told Jessi and Shannon what was going on, and then we walked Sean upstairs. On the way, we passed Logan, Claudia, and Stacey, but we didn't stop to talk. I knew it would be obvious to them that Sean was our firebug.

In Mrs. Kishi's office, Sean did begin to cry. He also confessed everything, since he knew he had been caught red-handed. "I'm sorry," he said, sniffling. "I know it was wrong to start those fires. I just did it because I hate being in the stupid Readathon. I don't even like to read, but my parents said I had to do it. They always want me and Corrie to do all these activities. Corrie doesn't mind — she *likes* taking ice-skating lessons and all that dumb stuff. I want to hang out at home, with my friends, but I'm never allowed to." By this time he was really crying. "Our parents just want us out of the way," he wailed.

Kristy and I exchanged glances. Sean was feeling ignored and abandoned, and he was obviously very mixed up about things. He was a kid who needed a lot of help, more than we could give him.

Mrs. Kishi thanked us and asked us to leave Sean with her. As we closed the door to her office Kristy and I heard her dialing the phone. "She must be calling his parents," said Kristy.

"I guess they won't be able to ignore him *now*," I said. I felt so awful for Sean that it was hard to be happy about the fact that we had solved the mystery. Still, it was a relief to know the library fires were a thing of the past. Our hard work had paid off.

CHAPTER 15

By the time Kristy and I were downstairs again, Mrs. Kishi had spoken to Ms. Feld over the intercom, telling her what had happened with Sean. Ms. Feld pulled me aside as I passed her desk. "I want to thank you and your friends for what you did," she said in a low voice. "I'm so glad this is finally over. I'd like to ask you not to talk about it while you're here, though, since I'd rather the other children not know about Sean." She shook her head and clucked her tongue. "Poor kid. You really have to feel sorry for someone who feels such a strong need for attention."

I passed on Ms. Feld's request to my friends. I had to stay and work for awhile, but Kristy and the others decided to leave. We agreed to talk about the day's events later on, during our meeting.

I spent the next hour or so trying to put what had happened out of my mind and just concentrate on my job. The Readathon would be ending in a few days, and the kids were frantic to finish up their reading. So I helped Charlotte pick out her last three books, and I tracked down a lost registration form for Sarah Hill. Luckily, the kids were so busy that none of them seemed to have noticed what had happened with Sean, so I didn't have to explain anything.

At about 5:10 I was on my way out of the library when Miss Ellway stopped me. "Such a pity about Sean," she said in a quiet voice. "But thank goodness he was caught before he did any real damage to this wonderful place."

I guessed Miss Ellway was okay, after all.

By the time I arrived at the BSC meeting, everybody else was already there. "Here she is!" said Stacey, as I hurried into Claud's room. "The greatest detective of the century!" Everybody clapped, and I gave a silly curtsy.

"Thank you, thank you," I said. "I couldn't have done it without my assistants, though."

Claudia passed out snacks: Ring-Dings and Ruffles, and bagel chips for Stacey. "And since it's a special occasion," she said, "I even have dip for the chips." She produced a bowl of onion dip, and we started to pig out.

Kristy called the meeting to order at five-thirty, and in between calls we talked about Sean and the fires. Mrs. Kishi had phoned

Claudia to tell her about her talk with Sean and his parents, and Claudia filled us in.

"Mr. and Mrs. Addison went right to the library," she reported. "Mom said there was a lot of hugging and crying going on."

"I never thought Mr. and Mrs. Addison ignored Sean," I said. "They seem like good parents."

"I agree," said Kristy. "But if Sean *felt* ignored, there's a problem."

"My mom said they talked about family therapy, and some special counseling for Sean," said Claudia. "Also, the police are involved, but I don't know what's going to happen with that. Sean's such a little kid."

"Still, it's a serious offense," said Stacey.

"Did Sean say anything else about the fires?" I asked Claud. "Did your mom find out anything about the fire at school?"

"The police said it was unrelated," Claud replied. "It was caused by a problem with electrical wiring."

"I guess we were way off track suspecting those book banners," mused Jessi. "I mean, I still don't believe in banning books, but at least they weren't *burning* them."

"We were off track with Miss Ellway, too," I added. "She's not so bad, after all. I think it just took her a while to get used to being around all those kids."

"What about Nicky?" asked Stacey. "He was a suspect, too — for awhile."

"Oh, right," said Claudia. "I forgot to mention that. Sean explained how those matches got into Nicky's pocket. See, he spotted them on the floor that day and realized they were his. He panicked, so he stuffed them into the nearest available hiding place. He felt really bad when he found out that the jacket belonged to Nicky."

"Whew!" I said. "I'm glad we believed Nicky when he told us they weren't his matches."

Kristy leaned back in her chair and tugged at her visor. "Well, the main thing is we don't have to worry about any more fires at the library," she said. "We can be happy about that."

I nodded, but somehow I wasn't feeling terribly happy.

"What's the matter, Mary Anne?" asked Claudia. "You look a little down."

"It's just that the Readathon is ending," I said. "It's been so much fun, and now it's almost over."

"You know," Claudia said, "Ms. Feld told my mom you're terrific with the kids. I bet she'd love for you to volunteer in the children's room once in awhile. You don't have to give up going there if you don't want to."

What a relief. I wouldn't have to go back to watching sad movies in the afternoons, after all. "That's great, Claud," I said. "Hey, you guys," I went on, "I hope you're planning to come to the Readathon awards ceremony on Saturday."

"We wouldn't miss it for the world," said Kristy.

Sure enough, by ten o'clock on Saturday morning, the members of the BSC were all on hand in the children's room. Even Mallory was there! Her parents had agreed to let her attend, after she and Nicky had begged them for the entire week.

I had arrived early to help set up chairs in the space near the puppet theatre. Ms. Feld was rushing around, getting ready for the ceremony. She laid out the certificates that would be given to the children who had participated, checked and double-checked her list of winners in each grade, and even had time to give last-minute quizzes to a couple of kids who had finished books just before the final deadline.

Miss Ellway and I helped seat the kids and their parents. Mr. and Mrs. Pike were there, along with all the Pike kids. I spotted Charlotte Johanssen and her parents, and Norman and Sarah Hill with their parents. The Arnolds were there, and so were the Sobaks and the Hobarts and the Braddocks. Even Sean and Corrie Addison were there with their parents. Mrs. Addison took me aside and thanked me for "helping out" with Sean. She kept her arm around him, and seemed to be giving him plenty of attention.

The children's room was noisier than I'd ever heard it, but when Ms. Feld stepped in front of the crowd, everybody quieted down. "Greetings!" she said. "We're so happy to have you here. I'd like to thank all the participants who made our Readathon such a success." Then she turned and smiled at me. "I would also like to thank Mary Anne Spier, who has been a tremendous help to me and Miss Ellway over these past weeks."

Everybody clapped, and I saw Nicky Pike stick his fingers into his mouth to give a loud whistle. I blushed.

"First of all, I'd like each of our readers to come up here as I call out your name. You can hand our volunteers," she gestured at two women sitting at the checkout desk, "the money you've earned, and they'll count it. We'll give you each a special Readathon certificate. After that, I'll tell you the total amount of money you earned, and then we'll announce the winners for most books read in each grade." She smiled around at the kids and parents. "This money will go toward some wonderful new books for our children's room, and I know you'll be proud to say you helped to buy them."

Again, there was applause. Then Ms. Feld began to call out names, and one by one the children came up to hand over their money. I have to confess I had a lump in my throat as I watched the kids march to the front of the room to turn in their money. And when Ms. Feld handed them their certificates, they smiled so proudly I had to work to hold back my tears. I knew Kristy would never let me forget it if she caught me crying at a Readathon ceremony.

Once the kids had received their certificates and were seated again, Ms. Feld took a few minutes to consult with the volunteers who had been counting the money. Then she turned back to the audience. "This is wonderful!" she said. "I know you'll all be proud and happy to hear that we raised even more money than we had expected to. We'll be able to buy quite a lot of new books." She announced the figure, and everybody applauded and cheered.

"All right," she said, as the cheering died down. "Now it's time to announce the winner in each grade. Our winners will receive these special coupons," she held up a handful of brightly colored papers, "for prizes donated by some of our local merchants." She picked up her list of winners and began to read. "Our first-grade winner is Mathew Hobart," she said. A big cheer arose as Mathew walked to the front of the room and shook Ms. Feld's hand. She handed him a green coupon, and he turned to display it to the crowd. He was grinning from ear to ear.

"The prize for most books read by a second-grader goes to Marilyn Arnold," announced Ms. Feld. Another cheer arose as Marilyn claimed her prize.

"I'm going to skip over the third-grade prize and come back to it, because it's a special one," said Ms. Feld. She smiled mysteriously. I looked around at the crowd, and noticed that Rosie Wilder was smiling, too. I figured she must have read so many books that she was going to get a special mention, along with her prize. As far as I knew, there was no question that she had read more books than any other third-grader.

"The fourth-grade prize goes to Sarah Hill," Ms. Feld said. Sarah, smiling shyly, stepped forward to receive her coupon. The crowd had barely stopped cheering when Ms. Feld announced the fifth-grade prize, which went to a boy I didn't know named Bruce Boyd.

"And now, the third-grade prize," said Ms.

Feld: "This prize is a special one because of the extra effort a certain person put into winning it. Can you all please join me in congratulating Nicky Pike, for reading the most books of any third-grader."

I was shocked — and I think a lot of other people in the audience were, too. Rosie Wilder turned pale, but then she recovered and yelled, "Yea, Nicky!" at the top of her lungs. Everybody else cheered, too, and I have to say the applause for Nicky was louder than the applause for any of the other winners. It didn't hurt that he had his own nine-member Pike family cheering section.

Nicky had to walk by me on his way to receive his coupon, and as he passed he leaned over and whispered in my ear, "Surprise!" He walked proudly to Ms. Feld, shook her hand, and accepted his coupon. Then he turned to the audience. "I just want to say that I worked hard because I wanted to win this prize for Mary Anne. I did most of my reading at home, so I could surprise her. She's the one who got me excited about reading. Thank you, Mary Anne!"

Okay, I admit it. That's where I lost it. I started to cry, and I didn't even try to hide it from Kristy. And when Charlotte yelled out, "Hooray for Mary Anne!" and the other kids started cheering, well — let's just say I ended up about as soggy as I had been after watching *Roman Holiday*. Luckily, at that moment a smiling Miss Ellway leaned over and handed me a clean, starched white handkerchief.

So, there you have it. I was a cry-baby *before* the Readathon, and I ended up sobbing at the end of it, too. But I wouldn't have missed it for anything. Fires and all, it was one of my best experiences ever.

A Note to Readers

Various groups have banned or tried to ban the books mentioned in this story from school and public libraries. For more information about book banning, contact the American Library Association, Office of Intellectual Freedom, 50 East Huron Street, Chicago, IL. (312) 944-6780.

About the Author

ANN M. MARTIN lives in New York City and loves animals, especially cats. She has two cats of her own, Mouse and Rosie.

Other books by Ann M. Martin that you might enjoy are *Stage Fright*; *Me and Katie (the Pest)*; and the books in *The Baby-sitters Club* series.

Ann likes ice cream and *I Love Lucy*. And she has her own little sister, whose name is Jane.

Look for Mystery #14

STACEY AND THE MYSTERY
AT THE MALL

Back at Toy Town, April was busy at the cash register, and there was a line of people waiting to be helped. "What can I do?" I asked.

She nodded toward the back of the store, where a boy was playing noisily near the train set. "Try to encourage him to use the display toys," she said. "I try to leave enough out, but the kids always go for the new stuff."

I walked back and discovered that the boy, who looked about eight, was tearing into a new package of Legos. "How about leaving those on the shelf?" I said.

He just stared at me.

I looked around for his mother. "Where's your mom?" I asked. "Or are you here with your dad? Or a baby-sitter?"

"My mom's shopping," the boy answered. "She said she'd be back soon."

I couldn't believe it. This boy's mother had

left him here, all by himself! I spent a few minutes getting him to help me clean up the Legos, and by the time we finished, his mother had turned up. "Have a good time, Jason?" she asked. She turned to me. "I always leave him here while I shop. He's happier, and I can be a lot more productive."

I watched her leave, shaking my head. April saw me, and smiled. "I know, it's awful," she said. "But it happens all the time, and what can I do? It's not like there's any better place to leave a kid while you shop." She shrugged. I was amazed she took it so well. The whole thing seemed crazy to me.

On the way home that afternoon, my friends and I talked about our first day on the job. I told my friends about Jason's mom leaving him at the store, and they were shocked — but not surprised. Mal had heard about the same thing happening at the bookstore, and Logan had even seen kids left at the food court.

I've always liked Washington Mall, and I loved my new job, but I was really beginning to wonder about a few things. Shoplifting, kids left alone. Working in the real world was an eye-opener.

**Read all the latest books
in the Baby-sitters Club series
by Ann M. Martin**

THE BABY-SITTERS CLUB ®

Mysteries

by Ann M. Martin

Something mysterious is going on in Stoneybrook, and now you can solve the case with the Baby-sitters! Collect and read these exciting mysteries along with your favorite Baby-sitters Club books!

THE BABY-SITTERS Club®

Hello, fans!

Although it's wintertime, it's never too early to think ahead to spring and this season Scholastic and I have come up with a special challenge just for you. We want all Baby-sitters Club fans to **GET INVOLVED!** Here's the challenge:

1. Think about an issue that matters to you and your community. It might be recycling or volunteering at a local hospital or shelter, or it might be something completely different! How would you get involved and help? Think about how the members of the Baby-sitters Club get involved, like Jessi when she works with the Kids Can Do Anything Club in JESSI'S WISH (#48). You can make a difference, too!

2. Write me a letter which describes, in 50 words or less, how you propose to **GET INVOLVED!** Tell me what's important to you about your selected cause and how you plan to take action.

3. Send in your letter. My assistants and I will be reading all the letters and selecting the ones which make an impact—letters we feel suggest the best and most creative ways to help others. More details about the prizes are included on the entry form.

I'm looking forward to hearing from you. When I was younger I was a candystriper at a local hospital and I later helped at a summer camp for handicapped children. Now that I'm older, I have a foundation which helps children and the homeless, and another foundation that creates children's libraries for kids who don't have easy access to books.

Even the smallest contribution matters—and getting involved can be an exciting adventure for you and your friends! So get set and **GET INVOLVED!**

Happy Writing!

Ann M. Martin

GET INVOLVED!
IT'S THE BABY-SITTERS CLUB ®

WINTER CHALLENGE!

If you're a BSC fan, you know that the Baby-sitters are always active and busy in their community...and not just with baby-sitting. When Stoneybrook needs help, the girls are ready to pitch in. If you're concerned about the town you live in, write a one-page letter about 50 words telling us your plan for improving it.

ENTER AND YOU CAN WIN:

GRAND PRIZE

• A $10,000 US Scholarship Savings Bond sponsored by Milton Bradley®, makers of The Baby-sitters Club Board Game and The Baby-sitters Club Mystery Game, and Kenner Products, makers of The Baby-sitters Club Dolls.

2 FIRST PRIZES

• A book dedicated to you, your cause and your community.
• A visit from Ann Martin to your hometown and local bookstore for an autographing and lunch.
• Plus..loads of quality BSC merchandise and a **BSC GET INVOLVED** sweatshirt, signed by Ann Martin.

100 RUNNERS-UP:
Win a **BSC GET INVOLVED** sweatshirt.

Just fill in the coupon below or write the information on a 3" x 5" piece of paper and mail with your "**GET INVOLVED**" letter to the appropriate address. U.S. Residents send entries to: **SCHOLASTIC INC., BSC WINTER CHALLENGE**, P.O. Box 742, Cooper Station, NY 10276. Canadian residents send entries to Iris Ferguson, Scholastic Inc., 123 Newkirk Road, Richmond Hill, Ontario, Canada LAC 3G5.

Rules: Entries must be postmarked by March 31, 1994. Winners will be judged by Scholastic Inc., and Ann M. Martin and notified by mail. No purchase necessary. Valid in the U.S. and Canada. Void where prohibited. Employees of Scholastic Inc., its agencies, affiliates, subsidiaries, and their immediate families are not eligible. For a complete list of winners, send a self-addressed stamped envelope after March 31, 1994. to: THE BSC WINTER CHALLENGE Winners List, at either address provided above.

- -

Attach this coupon to your **GET INVOLVED!** Letter.
THE BABY-SITTERS CLUB WINTER CHALLENGE

Name _____ Birthdate _____

Address _____ Phone# _____

City _____ State/Zip _____

Where did you buy this book? ☐ Bookstore ☐ Other (Specify) _____

Name of Bookstore _____

HAVE YOU JOINED THE BSC FAN CLUB YET! See back of this book for details.

BSC993

Don't miss out on
The All New

Fan Club

Join now!
Your one-year membership package includes:

- The exclusive Fan Club T-Shirt!
- A Baby-sitters Club poster!
- A Baby-sitters Club note pad and pencil!
- An official membership card!
- The exclusive *Guide to Stoneybrook!*

Plus four additional newsletters per year

so you can be the first to know the hot news about the series — Super Specials, Mysteries, Videos, and more — the baby-sitters, Ann Martin, and lots of baby-sitting fun from the Baby-sitters Club Headquarters!

ALL THIS FOR JUST $6.95 plus $1.00 postage and handling! **You can't get all this great stuff anywhere else except THE BABY-SITTERS FAN CLUB!**

Just fill in the coupon below and mail with payment to: THE BABY-SITTERS FAN CLUB, Scholastic Inc., P.O. Box 7500, 2931 E. McCarty Street, Jefferson City, MO 65102.

THE BABY-SITTERS FAN CLUB

___ YES! Enroll me in The Baby-sitters Fan Club! I've enclosed my check or money order (no cash please) for $7.95

Name _____ Birthdate _____

Street _____

City _____ State/Zip _____

Where did you buy this book?

❑ Bookstore	❑ Drugstore	❑ Supermarket
❑ Book Fair	❑ Book Club	❑ other_____

BSFC593

Create Your Own
Mystery Stories!

MYSTERY GAME!

WHO:	Boyfriend	**WHY:**	Romance
WHAT:	Phone Call	**WHERE:**	Dance

Use the special Mystery Case card to pick WHO did it, WHAT was involved, WHY it happened and WHERE it happened. Then dial secret words on your Mystery Wheels to add to the story! Travel around the special Stoneybrook map gameboard to uncover your friends' secret word clues! Finish four baby-sitting jobs and find out all the words to win. Then have everyone join in to tell the story!

NOW PLAYING!

Home Video Collection

*Look for these
all new episodes!*

■

**Claudia and the Mystery
of the Secret Passage**

Dawn Saves the Trees

The Baby-sitters and the Boy Sitters

**Jessi and the Mystery
of the Stolen Secrets**

Stacey Takes a Stand

The Baby-sitters Remember

■

*Available wherever fun
videos are sold.*

For More Information Call: 1-800-628-3100